dirty in
cashmere

dirty in cashmere
peter plate
a novel

SEVEN STORIES PRESS
New York • Oakland

Seven Stories Press
140 Watts Street
New York, NY 10013
sevenstories.com

Library of Congress Cataloging-in-Publication Data

Plate, Peter.
  Dirty in cashmere : a novel / Peter Plate. -- First Seven Stories Press edition.
    pages ; cm
  ISBN 978-1-60980-617-0 (softcover : acid-free paper)
  1. Prophets--Fiction. 2. Dystopias--Fiction. 3. San Francisco (Calif.)--Fiction. I. Title.
  PS3566.L267D57 2015
  813'.54--dc23
                                2014038376

Printed in the United States of America

9 8 7 6 5 4 3 2 1

COVER IMAGE CREDIT:
Gottfried Helnwein, *The Disasters of War 13*, 2007
Mixed media on canvas, 70 ¾" x 50 ½"
Courtesy of the artist and Modernism Inc., San Francisco
Image copyright: Gottfried Helnwein 2007

Nostalgia doesn't live here anymore.
—graffiti on Market Street

THE FIRST WEEK

ONE

In late October, three days before the month's end, black rain bombarded the streets of San Francisco, overrunning curbs, spilling onto the sidewalk next to Eternal Gratitude, a squat, flat-roofed club at the intersection of Church and Market.

2-Time Wright straddled a stool by Eternal Gratitude's sandbagged plywood front door. He sported a yellow T-shirt, chinos that exaggerated the cleft of his high buttocks, a vintage Giants baseball hat with the bill pulled low over his pasty face.

He heard the doorbell, a high-pitched squeal that rattled the aluminum mesh security gate, glanced up, saw me standing outside in the downpour. I had on no-label jeans. My kicks were blinding white Nike knockoffs, ten bucks at the Oakland flea market. A vermilion scar glowered on my forehead.

He jeered at me. "What the hell do you want?"

Sorely troubled by how the rain was messing with

my hair, I weighed 2-Time's question. I toyed with the notion of imagining his future. But with certain dudes, you didn't want to bother. 2-Time was one of those cats.

"I'm here to buy some Life."

"Okay, man, go in and make your purchase. But if you cause any trouble in my establishment, I will kick your ass."

The sound system was delivering Howlin' Wolf's "Going Down Slow" when I stepped into the narrow and low-ceilinged club. Wall lamps emitted a dim light. My shoes sank into ersatz Turkish carpets piled three deep on the oak plank floor. I was the only customer in the place.

2-Time's spouse Rita, a slender woman with shoulder-length peroxided hair, demurely attired in a floral-patterned muumuu, was working the cash register. Enormous glass jars brimming with double-barreled white tabs of Life dominated a laminated counter.

Life was the street name of the new experimental radiation vaccine invented after the Fukushima nuclear disaster in Japan in March 2011, when contamination spread across the Pacific Ocean to California. A delay in patenting the drug had boomeranged into an underground market. Life was manufactured in neighborhood laboratories and distributed in local storefront clubs sanctioned by the mayor's office. Eternal Gratitude was a small operation, run by 2-Time and Rita. Unlike most clubs that retailed Life, it wasn't making money. Competition was stiff. The overhead was high.

Rita eyed me as I sauntered to the counter. This was the second consecutive day I'd come by. She was delighted to see me again. Business had been slow for a Monday afternoon. She switched on her sales face.

"Can I help you?"

I pointed at a jar. "Give me three tabs, please."

"Is there anything else I can get you?"

"Nope. Just three tabs."

"That's seventy bucks."

I had my money out and was counting scruffy one dollar bills, moving my lips as I added up the numbers. Seventy bones was a lot to pay for Life. I laid the paper by the cash register. Rita noticed the scarring on my forehead.

"Where did you get that scar? It's so damn big."

Ten months ago I was shot in the head at the corner of Geneva and Mission by a vigilante from the Citizens' Council, a civilian organization that patrolled crime-ridden neighborhoods. My heart stopped four times during the ambulance ride to General Hospital. The surgeons in the trauma unit concluded I was brain dead. I was hooked up to a life support system in a sterile room. Thirty-six weeks passed while I was in a coma and then, without any fanfare, I emerged from it. The doctors told me they couldn't remove the bullet. It would kill me if they tried. That's when I began having visions. Perceiving things. The bullet had become a third eye.

"I was shot in the head."

"That's fucking sick! Do you know who did it?"

"A vigilante."

I could see it in her eyes. She thought I was a bullshit artist. Her standard for credibility was 2-Time, a man who probably lied all the time.

"Was he arrested?"

"Nah. And he won't be. Not in this lifetime."

"Why not?"

"The police said he shot me in self-defense."

"What were you doing to him?"

"Nothing. I was just walking by."

"When did this happen?"

"January."

"Are you okay?"

"Better than I used to be. I can see all kinds of things now, stuff I never saw before."

"You got a crystal ball or something?"

I pictured the bullet in my brain, gray and pitted, always giving me advice about the future and everything else. "More than that."

"What is it you see?"

"Everything people do. Like with this club." I looked around Eternal Gratitude. "You're going to go bankrupt."

"What's your name?"

"Ricky Bellamy."

Still at the door, 2-Time overheard every word I said. I knew what he was thinking: if I could see Eternal Gratitude's economic future, there wasn't anything I couldn't see. I was the ultimate lottery ticket. Movies. Radio. Television. Advertising deals. Lecture circuit. Anyone associating with me would make paper.

But if 2-Time wanted a piece of the action, he knew he'd have to move fast. Like pronto. And so he backpedaled out of Eternal Gratitude, cell phone in hand.

I pocketed the three tabs of Life. I told Rita I'd come back tomorrow. I followed 2-Time out the door.

Something about how 2-Time walked, his prison-style swagger, grabbed my attention.

I called out to him, "2-Time, did you get punked in jail?"

He threw a shocked glance at me, his face deadly white.

I'd pinpointed his darkest secret.

TWO

I walked on Market Street to Van Ness Avenue, ambling past the homeless winos camping by the Civic Center Hotel. Two men were boiling noodles in a pot over a sterno can. They looked at me, as if I were contaminated. But I wasn't. I'd tested negative.

The rain was coming down; pools of water shimmered white on the asphalt. Ever since I got shot, I'd had a constant loud ringing in my ears. The doctors said it was from neurological damage. The noise in the street amplified it. I hunched my shoulders and humped it to Mission Street. At a bus stop I boarded an outbound 14 Mission coach. I heard a small girl ask her mother, "Why does everyone look so scared?"

The bus highballed down the street. With half-closed eyes I drank in elderly crackheads levitating over the sidewalk and Salvadoreno ice cream vendors pushing carts under palm trees gray from smog. Forty-five minutes later at the corner of Geneva and Mission, jostling with junior high kids in backpacks and Asian women carting shopping bags, I alighted from the coach.

I scoped the corner, the shops, the baleful stoplights, the traffic moving in the street. I scanned the cracked concrete at my feet, fifty yards from Acme Surplus. This was where I was dusted. There should've been a shrine, an altar. Something to mark the spot. There wasn't even a bloodstain. Nothing to let me know a crime-crazed vigilante had gunned me down here on a foggy night in the first week of the new year.

I patted my shirt pocket, the tabs of Life were still there. I started west on Geneva, past stucco homes, each one a tiny continent of anonymity, a fine metallic mist in the air. The rain blinded me, the wind slid over my wet hair. My arms swung back and forth. Everything seemed to be working just fine. But the bullet pulsed in my head. It was like the sun. The rest of my body circled around it; my legs and arms, dick and stomach were planets in orbit. Except that my left leg had a tendency to drift off on its own, forcing me to limp.

I lurched to Guadalupe Terrace, a short one-way lane that dead-ended behind the Balboa Park BART station. Giant tumbleweeds crisscrossed the roadbed. Newspapers, tin cans, beer bottles, fast food wrappers, eggshells, and rotting banana peels nested against the curb, secure in the knowledge they'd be there for many months.

A trio of abandoned houses hugged the sidewalk, starting with a boarded up pastel blue bungalow that a pair of Honduran kids had turned into a Life manufacturing lab. The next building was a rundown pseudo-Moorish confection occupied by a black skinhead girl.

My cottage was the last on the block. It had a white paint job and a red-tiled roof. Since the front and back doors were nailed shut, I had to climb in the broken kitchen window to get inside. I wriggled through the window, dropped to the floor and sat there. The kitchen had no chairs, no table, not even a sink or a stove.

I pulled the tabs of Life from my shirt pocket, stuck all three in my mouth, chewed them, gulped. Reaching in my pants for a packet of papers and a pouch of tobacco, I subtracted a leaf, dropped some loose tobacco on it, glued it together. I lighted the rollup and in the process, ignited my shirt. I swatted the fire, bringing it under control.

I tried to remember my past, but it was difficult with the bullet in me. The past was just fragments of memory, shrapnel, a jumble of things mostly forgotten. Yet I remembered when I was near death. First, a white light engulfed me. After that was the welcoming committee. My mother was leading it. Trailing behind her was my dad.

My father was among the youngest men ever sent to a maximum security penitentiary in California. He was sixteen, sentenced as an adult for stealing and selling guns. The first time he was released from the slammer he married my mom. He later returned to the joint and died in a hunger strike at Pelican Bay.

The vaccine made me woozy. My muscles went liquid, the snakes of pain in my head uncoiled. I sniffled, wiped my nose, shut my eyes, nodded off.

THREE

As I slept I dreamed that 2-Time was chatting to one of his confederates about me. I felt like I was eavesdropping on a conversation.

While 2-Time yakked a blue streak, his buddy Rance Heller gazed out his office window and felt sorry for himself. The gaudy red and yellow pennants that decorated his South Van Ness Avenue used car lot drooped in the rain. Rows of beat Chevy and Ford sedans sat idle on the wet gravel.

2-Time was blabbing that I could augur the future. What better fairy tale than a teenager who could see the future? Heller thought 2-Time was out of his fucking gourd.

A while back Heller got strung out on angel dust from partying with 2-Time. He ended up doing a year in county jail for possession with intent to sell. Thanks to his wife Mitzi and the 12-step program, he was now clean. Unfortunately, 2-Time was still doing angel dust.

Even though Heller was the silent partner behind Eternal Gratitude, the two men were no longer close friends.

"You're telling me this kid Ricky Bellamy who got shot in the head knows the future?"

2-Time's lawnmower rasp shredded Heller's ear. "Fuck, yeah."

"What is he, a swami?"

"Yup. He told Rita that Eternal Gratitude was going bankrupt."

"That's my point, dork. I could've told you that. Anyone could. That's nothing. You still don't know shit about what he can do. How do you know he can really tell the future? Maybe he was talking trash."

"No way. He knows things about me I wish he didn't."

"He still has to prove himself. You talk to him and we'll test his powers."

"Okay."

They agreed to meet tomorrow. 2-Time promised to bring me. Heller hung up the phone. He was mildly excited. Whoever manipulated the future, got all the money. It was the oldest law in history. The second oldest law was just as important. You never trusted scuzzballs like 2-Time.

I awoke with my face bathed in greasy sweat. What I'd overheard was no dream. Far from it.

FOUR

I was in a daze that Tuesday afternoon as I tramped up Market Street to Eternal Gratitude. On one side of the street construction cranes towered over half-finished apartment buildings. Bevies of sparrows cavorted above the power lines. A billboard by a Whole Foods store asked:

DEPRESSED? LESIONS?
CONTAMINATION GOT YOU DOWN?
CALL THE DEPARTMENT OF PUBLIC HEALTH
415-863-3486.

In front of me was a strangely familiar man, a heavy shouldered blond fellow in matching black Carhartt coat and jeans. I swore it was Frank Blake, the vigilante who'd shot me. I quickened my pace to catch up with his fat ass. But when I drew abreast of him, it wasn't anyone I'd ever seen before. My father's ghost jabbered inside my head, warning me to be careful. All around me the traffic in the street was a rising crescendo that threatened to over-whelm everything with its self-important cacophony.

"Ricky Bellamy! Just the man I want to see!"

2-Time jackknifed from his doorway stool, thrilled that I'd returned to the club because Tuesday was turning out as slow as Monday.

I was dragging my left leg. It bothered me today. The bullet was hurting, too. I chalked it up to the weather. The fog lay low, hepatic yellow rain clouds were on the horizon.

2-Time hustled me into the club, nudged me over to the counter. The air was dusty and I sneezed. "It's good that you're here," he warbled. "We have serious shit to talk about."

From her nook behind the cash register, Rita smiled at me, but not at her husband. Her head was angled, so that only I received the benediction of her upturned lips. "Hello, Ricky. How are you?"

I was matter of fact. "I'm hurting like a motherfucker."

"Do you want something to help with that?"

"Shit, yeah. I need some medicine."

"You heard him," 2-Time mewled at Rita. "Show him the good stuff."

Rita went to the basement to locate the high-grade Life, the kind that made your thyroid levels stay normal. While I waited for her, I surveyed the other products for sale in the club. There were handcrafted tabs from Mendocino. Tablets manufactured in San Mateo. There were some from Mexico.

"Listen, homey." 2-Time propped himself against the counter, chewing on a toothpick. "I want to see how you tell the future."

I focused on his face. 2-Time didn't cotton to how I stared at him without blinking. It unnerved him. He talked around the toothpick. "You've got a special talent. You need to use it."

I stifled the compulsion to tell 2-Time to shut his mouth. I decided to flow with the flow, to see what happened next.

2-Time made his pitch. "I can do things for you to advance your career. I know people."

I wasn't impressed. I knew people, too. Too many people. All I wanted to do was go back to Guadalupe Terrace and take Life until the snakes of pain in my head stopped slithering around.

"The future is money," piped 2-Time. "But you have to have proper guidance to get it. Folks that can market your ass." 2-Time laid the bait and set the trap. "I know a cat who can do it. His name is Rance Heller." 2-Time's falsetto ping-ponged off the club's walls. "He's an entrepreneur. Top shelf."

I was receptive to 2-Time's hype. If he thought I was an oracle, that was okay by me. "He wants to see me?"

"Hell, yeah. You're the kid who can tell the future. You should be on television. In Las Vegas. Even at the White

House." 2-Time worked his juju on me. "Rance is dying for you to meet with us."

"I'm okay with that."

"How about this afternoon?"

"Sure. That's cool."

2-Time was pleased, but concealed his happiness behind a mask of indifference. I think he felt good to wear indifference on his face. Like a beautiful woman wearing exquisite makeup.

Rita came back to the counter. In her arms was a glass jar filled with sparkling white double-barreled tablets. "Here's the good shit. Only eighty for three."

I frowned. "Eighty bucks for three tabs?"

"That's with the discount. Because today is customer appreciation day."

"Fuck it." I scratched my chin. "I'll take them."

Rita shortchanged me half a tab, which was the club's normal policy. I gave her four twenties. I knew she found me compelling. She loved my terrible scar and my quiet manner, so unlike her husband. I palmed the tabs, turned around without saying good-bye and pulled my troubled leg toward the exit. 2-Time brayed at me from the counter: "I'll see you in a couple of hours, dude."

I was at the bus stop, just standing there, when I saw Vivian Raleigh, the girl who'd taken my virginity. I hadn't seen her since I got shot. She saw me too and turned her moist brown eyes in my direction. How I remembered those eyes. When she was warm and loving, they were dark brown. Eyes that soaked in all the light surrounding them. But when she was alienated, they were pale brown. At this moment they were almost yellow.

Vivian had on platform shoes that gave her a six-inch advantage in height over me, sharply creased bell bottoms, and a belted coat. Her kinky black hair swelled in the rain. A symphony of expressions rippled across her sculpted, high-cheeked face. Fondness. Bemusement. Alarm. Indifference. Each emotion was buried under its successor. She spoke, out of politeness. "Hey, Ricky. Long time, no see."

"I've been busy."

"You look different. Smaller."

By talking with Vivian Raleigh I'm exercising a personal tradition: seeking tenderness in the wrong people. Vivian slept with tons of guys after we broke up. It was an effective technique to get rid of every trace of me, not only on her body but inside her heart. I wasn't even a historical point of reference in her life. But me? I hadn't been with anyone since her. I'd been in the hospital.

"How'd you get that scar on your face? It's hideous."

If Vivian hadn't heard about my misfortune, I wasn't going to broadcast it. "I had an accident. I'm better now."

She gave me a toothsome smile that said she didn't believe me. I'd heard she was dating a big dope dealer and going to the Marinello Schools of Beauty. Serendipitously, my bus pulled up at the stop. I was grateful. It was nasty seeing her.

"I'll talk to you later, Vivian."

FIVE

I journeyed down the hill on Geneva and turned onto Guadalupe Terrace. The steady, reliable hum of the Hondurans' laboratory generator seeped into the street. My neighbor, the skinhead girl, hailed me from her porch. "Hey, wait!"

I stiffened, kept walking. The girl bounded down the porch steps and across a desiccated front lawn, cutting me off on the sidewalk.

She was diminutive, in a plaid miniskirt, torn black stockings, oxblood Doc Martens, a soiled red T-shirt, cartoon tattoos on her arms. Her hair was shorn to the scalp, except for a shock of dyed red bangs that hung over her eyes, which were bright black and fixed on me. She held a perspiring bottle of Bud in one hand. She waved the bottle at me by way of a greeting. "Who the fuck are you?"

I looked down at my kicks.

"Ricky Bellamy."

"Can you tell me why you look so weird?"

"I was shot by a goddamn vigilante."

"That's wicked."

I confessed in an asthmatic slur. "I almost died." I hopped from one foot to the other. "What do they call you?"

"Spike."

"You out here all by yourself?"

"Yeah. How long you been staying next door?"

"Three days. Since I got out of the hospital."

"You got any parents?"

"They're dead. How about you?"

"Same."

I envisaged Spike's destiny. Cosmetic school. Two kids and a spouse who drove trucks for a living. A tract house in Daly City. Laser surgery to remove her tattoos. It was a decent fate. No unnecessary drama. I was relieved.

I enjoyed talking to her, the monosyllabic repartee volleying to and fro between us. I rotated my neck to get a crick out of it. The bullet didn't relish the movement and protested. I winced hard.

Spike caught the gesture.

"What's wrong?"

"The bullet hurts."

"What bullet?"

"The one in my head."

"They didn't take it out?"

"No. It'd kill me if they did."

She assayed me with newfound respect. "Harsh."

Out of nowhere, I got nervous. The rehab specialists at the hospital said it would happen. That I'd feel occasionally uncomfortable. They told me it was a post-traumatic stress disorder. It was more than that. Getting shot? That just honed the fact I'd always been afraid.

"I have to go."

I departed for my bombed out cottage. Once I was inside it, I settled down in the kitchen, a room that was more comfortable than the others, which were trashed with holes in the ceilings, walls, and floors. I lay down on my side and listened to unseen mice scurrying. My stomach was empty. I couldn't remember when I'd eaten. Not that it mattered. My appetite was nothing. Another thing that was nothing was 2-Time's scheme. I didn't want to be in Las Vegas. I wanted none of that. I just needed money.

I started to float away, my mind going to dark places. I watched the sky, shadowed by a cream cheese frieze of clouds, all of it framed in the kitchen window. I didn't trust 2-Time. Not one bit. 2-Time was a minor league con man. A snake in the grass.

SIX

I was leaving my place for the meeting with 2-Time and
Heller when I had a seizure. I pitched to the ground and
clawed the yard's dirt, my legs kicking the earth. My hands
and feet tingled. An electrical feeling moved through my
dick into my guts, over my chest and to my head, where
it exploded into a cavalcade of red lights behind my eyes,
making the bullet go bananas. Foam bubbled on my
chapped lips. I screamed at God to help me.

"Where are you, motherfucker?"

Nobody came to my rescue.

A half hour later I lugged myself into Eternal Gratitude.
Rita tooled out from behind the counter to meet me. She
was in a green leather miniskirt, sleeveless blue silk blouse,
black mules. 2-Time was right on her heels. Wearing the
same yellow T-shirt caked with deodorant stains.

"Let's hit it. Rance is waiting for you and me."

Rance Heller lived in a rent-controlled three-story fire-
trap tenement walkup on Woodward Street, a hundred

yards south of the crosstown freeway. He and his wife Mitzi were among the few white people on the block, the rest being Samoans, Filipinos and Mexicans. He was well known, having sold used cars and Life to everybody in the area.

When 2-Time and myself arrived at Heller's crib, the first thing 2-Time did was introduce me to Heller and Mitzi. Heller was a lanky man with straight graying hair and a lush mouth permanently ready to crack a false smile. The disappointment he felt upon seeing me was naked. Any hopes he had of getting rich died on the spot. I was nothing but a scrawny kid with untamed, wind-blown hair. I was no seer.

Heller smirked at us.

"I'm glad you guys came over."

Heller's mood deteriorated even further when his wife started flirting with me. A short brunette profiling a spotty white complexion and darting green eyes that never settled on anything, Mitzi burned with the self-awareness of a sexually charismatic woman, tilting her shoulders whenever she wanted to charm me, a gesture offset by how coldly she gazed at her husband.

We were seated in the living room. Smooth jazz was on the radio. George Benson playing guitar. Mitzi had on a sheer blue dress that made it plain her breasts were unencumbered by a bra. She challenged me, talking with the stretched out consonant and vowel drawl of most young people in the neighborhood.

"How come you never blink?"

I stared at her chest. "I was shot. I have a bullet in my head."

Heller interrupted us. "That's how he sees the future. Now he's going to show us his talent. Let's start with a simple test. Ricky? Every week I buy a hundred bucks in lottery tickets from the liquor store at Fourteenth and Valencia. I've never won more than a single penny. Will I win next week?"

My response was decisive. "No."

Heller's mood lightened. Now he was getting somewhere. If nothing else, I was a money saver. "That's splendid. I want you and 2-Time to come with me to the window."

The three of us went to the window, which overlooked Woodward Street. Down on the sidewalk, several dudes loitered by a parked car. One of them, a heavyset Honduran, held a brown paper bag. Heller pointed him out to me.

"See that guy? He sells unlicensed Life. Every day he collects money from those other guys. So let me ask you. Does he have money in the bag now?"

I said what Heller wanted to hear.

"Yeah."

"Can you predict whether he'll have money later today?"

"He will."

"Will it be the same amount?"

"Maybe more."

Heller exulted. Bingo. I was a goldmine.

2-Time looked at me with admiration. I had passed the test. I was a genius. Because he knew the fastest route to large amounts of cash was to steal it, and I was going to light the way.

A warm feeling oozed down my neck into my shoulders before coming to rest in my stomach where it fizzed with a pleasant sensation. But the good feeling rapidly dissipated into a spearpoint of nausea. Heller and 2-Time didn't intend to get me on television or into Las Vegas. Not even. I was a compass to help them rip off vaccine money.

"We done here?" I whined.

Heller preened. "Absolutely not. This is the start of a fantastic relationship."

SEVEN

It didn't take long for Heller and 2-Time to expedite my prediction. At half past five on the same day, they veered around the corner onto Fourteenth Street. One minute, they were on Mission Street, luxuriating in the sun's dubious warmth. The next minute, they were in the shadow of the fortress-like Mission Armory, freezing their balls off.

"Wait up," 2-Time hissed at Heller. "You're walking too fast."

Heller kept his eyes on the Honduran in front of them—the cat in oversized jeans, a worn flannel shirt, Timberland boots, designer sunglasses, and carrying a large black canvas bag. Heller started walking faster. His heart pounded right next to the Glock in his coat pocket. He whistled a tune, something from Aretha Franklin, "You Make Me Feel Like a Natural Woman." Taking a deep breath, he filled his nostrils with unclean autumn air. He drew the Glock, letting it dangle by his side, close to his leg. Now he was fifty feet from the Honduran, a hundred feet from the next stoplight.

He was determined to make contact before the light. He had to. 2-Time was on edge, his nerves perpetually shot from angel dust. At any given moment, he could fuck up and spoil things. The proof was how he was doing business at Eternal Gratitude. How could anyone lose money on Life? Somehow, 2-Time had managed the impossible.

There was another problem, too. The robbery itself. Heller and 2-Time were taking down a Life dealer in their own neighborhood. They were shitting in their own nest. It wasn't kosher. People died for less.

Too bad, thought Heller.

The Honduran stopped to light a cigarette. Heller strolled up to him and jammed the gun in his neck, the muzzle biting several folds of flab. The Honduran cocked his arm, swung it, burying the freshly lit cigarette in Heller's left cheek, extinguishing the cherry.

Howling in pain, Heller raked the Glock's barrel across the Honduran's nose, pulping it, then backhanded him several times in the chin, building a tempo. When the tempo was where he wanted it, he snagged the bag. Heller executed a rapid about-face and collided into 2-Time, which almost caused him to drop the loot. He shoved 2-Time in the chest.

"Get the fuck away from me, you maggot!"

The two thieves hoofed it south on Julian Avenue.

Heller hugged the stolen bag. The money rustling inside the sack made a seductive sound. It was music to his ears. Worth the hellacious cigarette burn on his face. He hooted over his shoulder at 2-Time, who lagged behind, "We're fucking rich!"

It was dusk on Woodward Street. The sky above the cross-town freeway was a bruised eggplant purple. In his walk-up's bedroom Heller counted the money, the bills spread on the floor. A small hummock of used hundreds. Forty thousand bucks.

Heller was thankful Mitzi wasn't home. She'd sink her teeth into the dough so fast, it'd be gone by tomorrow. His next thought was less charitable: how and when to steal 2-Time's portion of the money.

The door opened. 2-Time slinked into the room, looked at Heller. There wasn't much to see. Just his buddy adorned with a righteous cigarette burn. The money was another issue. It lay on the rug like Christ in the manger, so perfect, virginal, and innocent. 2-Time was leery to touch the cash, afraid it was a mirage. He wiped his runny nose. "What is Bellamy's share?"

"Who?"

"Don't give me that shit. The kid, that's who. How much is his cut?"

"For doing what?"

"He led us to the money, in case you forgot. We have to give him, uh, a finder's fee, or whatever."

"There's forty thousand here. Let's give him four hundred."

"That much?"

Heller smiled. 2-Time was so cute.

Cheating me wouldn't be as cute. Not when I found out I was getting shafted. Heller wasn't too concerned. He was confident he could manipulate me. He thought I was so naive and stupid, it was laughable.

EIGHT

On Wednesday morning 2-Time, Heller, Rita, and myself were barricaded inside Eternal Gratitude. A banner inscribed with the winning phrase VOTED BEST LIFE CLUB IN SAN FRANCISCO was tacked to the wall above the cash register. 2-Time had forged the slogan. Eternal Gratitude had won nothing.

Rita was behind the counter, loading tabs into a bag. The club had recently expanded its services to include home deliveries. Since Rita and 2-Time had no car, deliveries were conducted by taxi, which added to Eternal Gratitude's overhead. To make matters worse, the landlord had called up and said he was raising the rent another four thousand bucks a month. Claiming other clubs had approached him and offered more money for the space. Church and Market was prime real estate.

Heller deadpanned at me. "Your cut from the job is four hundred bucks."

"What the fuck." I was flummoxed. "That's all?"

"Correct."

"Four hundred?"

Heller's mouth looked like a knife wound. He opened it and no blood came out, but the words he said were just as ugly. "Yeah, four hundred. Why? Because you were wrong. You fucked up. The guy you spotted, the one with the money? He didn't have shit. He had nothing. Only fifteen hundred measly bucks. Your share is fair. Me and 2-Time are doing right by you."

A stew of emotions boiled across my face. Heller was literate when it came to facial vocabulary. He saw my despair and self-doubt cooking at a high flame and decided to capitalize on it. "Don't sweat it. This was just a test run."

"A test run? What do you mean?"

"You want to make money? It's not easy."

"I never thought it was."

"It could get tough."

"I know that."

"We have to do it again." Heller honeyed his voice until it was sweet and inviting with the merest hint of malevolence. "Me and 2-Time did our part. Now you've got to do yours. Better."

2-Time added his opinion to Heller's opinion. This was his chance to shine. "He's onto something, Ricky. You might have some talent, but you need to refine your chops. More practice and shit. You're not slick yet."

"I'm not?" My scar turned deep red from embarrassment.

"No, you're not," Heller butted in. "You failed. I'll bet you've heard that before. A kid like you."

"You don't know me."

"I know what it's like having no money. But there's a way to get some more."

"All right, all right." I glared at Heller. The punk was boondoggling me. The thing of it was, I was in a bind. I needed cash fast. "I'll make another prediction later today."

Heller absently fingered his cigarette burn. "Hallelujah."

Late that afternoon I sat on top of Bernal Hill. The sky was laced with black contrails. Below me, the city was spread out in a grid to Diamond Heights. Off to my left was St. Luke's Hospital in the Mission. Further off was Mount Sutro. To my right was China Basin and the Bay Bridge.

No matter how I concentrated, I couldn't predict my own future. Something stopped me. It wasn't forgetfulness. A piece of my mind was missing in action. Someday, I'd ask the bullet where it had gone.

A sudden noise exploded in the nearby oleander bushes—a coyote shot out from the undergrowth and thrashed downhill. I got to my feet, shook the dirt from my pants, and followed the coyote down the hillside to Mission Street.

I was tired when I got to my house. I took a tab of Life and snuggled on the kitchen floor. I fell asleep and dreamed my old dog Butch got run over by a car.

Butch was splattered in the street, right on the yellow dividing line. I went to look at him. The neighbors were there. One of them said: "We need to put Butch out of his misery."

The man went away and came back with a shotgun. He stood over the wounded mutt and pointed the gun. He fired once. The impact lifted Butch an inch off the ground.

I woke up from the nightmare with a jolt. I didn't go back to sleep. The rest of the afternoon sneaked away like a thief.

NINE

At Eternal Gratitude a spate of rare sunshine anointed the skylights, suffusing the club's interior with uncommon brightness. Rita dumped a jar of tablets onto the counter. Today was inventory day. The tabs needed counting. The triple-beam weight scales needed polishing. The chill out room up front needed airing—a customer had complained it was moldy.

Performing her chores, Rita replayed the movie she'd seen that morning. The movie starring 2-Time, Heller, and me. How her husband and Heller had cheated me. Telling me there was no real payoff from the robbery.

But the truth was, with the landlord's recent demand for higher rent, Eternal Gratitude's destiny was bleak. An extra four thousand a month? There was no damn way they could afford the hike without augmenting their income.

The rent problem was insignificant compared to the rumor she'd heard earlier. The word on the street was that too much Life was flooding the city. Prices were sinking. This meant purgatory for Eternal Gratitude.

I was their only hope. If I made a couple of slick predictions—abracadabra and all that shit—the rent would get paid. Then again, maybe it was a pipe dream. Me and the future.

"Rita!" 2-Time boomed from the cellar, aborting her reverie. "Five bags of tabs are missing. Do you know where they are? I can't remember."

That was the problem with Life—the vaccine's short term memory loss factor was high. 2-Time remembered what he did five years ago better than what he did yesterday. Life also gave him the shakes, similar to early onset Parkinson's disease.

2-Time emerged from the basement, toting a garbage bag of tabs. He heaved the sack on the counter, stopped to glance at his wife. The blankness on Rita's face disturbed him. She was standing by the cash register, spacing out. In 2-Time's opinion, Rita spaced out too often.

He was vexed. "Where the fuck is Bellamy?"

2-Time thought about his twenty grand. Soon, there would be more money. A magic mountain of cash.

TEN

The telephone had been ringing nonstop for ten minutes. Heller paid no attention to it. He was in bed with Mitzi. Taking it easy. Yet he was depressed. The next job he and 2-Time had up their sleeves was a doozy. It was a big target, five times larger than the last one. That meant the heist was five times riskier. Somebody might get killed.

My first prediction had been successful. That made Heller nervous. Maybe it had been a fluke. Beginner's luck. Who knew? And I bugged him. Why should a nineteen-year-old kid know the future? It wasn't fair. Heller had no such power. It made him sad.

All the months he'd spent backing Rita and 2-Time's venture at Eternal Gratitude was even more depressing to him. It'd been precious investment capital down the drain.

Brooding, he looked out the window. A raven flitted over the telephone lines, black wings glinting opalescent white against the tarred rooftops. He looked at Mitzi. It wasn't hard to do when she had no clothes on. With her heart-shaped ass, toned legs, and flat stomach, Mitzi was a hot number. A surefire guarantee their marriage wouldn't last. How could it? He was fifteen years older than her.

To complicate everything, the cigarette burn on his face wasn't healing. He'd gone last night to the emergency room at General Hospital. The doctor on duty prescribed antibiotics. Heller was avoiding mirrors.

Mitzi crawled over to him, looped her arms around his unshaven neck. "We're rich, daddy."

He hated it when she called him daddy. What was he, some kind of fucking geriatric? He was only thirty-eight, for Christ's sake.

Mitzi beamed at him with slightly crossed eyes. "What are you thinking?"

Heller's other concern was 2-Time. He was fed up with him. Rita, he could take in small doses. Whatever her faults, which were myriad, at least she didn't do angel dust. That was one small, but significant blessing. Most important was 2-Time's money. Heller still intended to help himself to it.

"Honey, I'm talking to you."

"Sorry." He was jarred from his funk. "I was meditating."

"On what?"

"Bellamy."

"He's really handsome."

"You think?" It was the last thing Heller wanted to hear. "He never blinks. He drags his leg when he walks."

"Shit, you're jealous."

Heller shifted onto his side, the better to scowl at Mitzi. She was getting on his nerves. He remembered how she flirted with Bellamy. It was something he ought to forget.

The telephone was still ringing. Heller lifted his heavy flanks out of bed, tied a sheet around his hips, plodded across the carpeted bedroom floor, crushing the stolen money underfoot. He waddled into the living room, grabbed the landline. "Yeah?"

"Rance?"

"What do you want, 2-Time?"

"Where is Bellamy?"

"How the hell do I know?"

"I'm worried about him. That hapless kid is walking around all by himself. What if we lose him? There goes the money."

"Relax."

"I can't, man. This shit is getting to me."

"Just try, okay?"

Heller hung up. He was amused. 2-Time should've known from the instant he met Bellamy, that things would get chaotic.

Mitzi tiptoed over to him, draped her arms around his neck, dug her newly painted orange fingernails into his back hair. "Who was that?"

"Nobody, baby." He purred like a kitten under her touch and prudently chose to remain vague. No ill-tempered comment would spring from his lips. "Just some fucking loser with the wrong number."

ELEVEN

"Don't you have any friends?"

I looked up, startled. Spike was at the hedge that divided my backyard from hers. She was styling a green nylon bomber jacket over a camisole, white stockings, and Doc Martens. Mascara was smudged around her bloodshot eyes. Her red bangs were stiff with gel, knife-like against her scalp.

Friendship was a sore point. Nobody came to see me when I was in the hospital. My friends avoided me. No one wanted to get close to death, in fear it might rub off on them, that they might be next.

"I'm an oracle. I don't have friends."

I'd been sitting in the overgrown grass behind the cottage for an hour, trying to figure out what to do. 2-Time and Heller wanted me to make another foretelling. I had qualms about that.

The events that were now taking place had nothing to do with what I was like before I was shot. But I'd nearly died.

And after you've been on the verge of death, living is different. Colors were brighter. Emotions were sharper. Almost unbearable.

Around dinnertime I shambled into Eternal Gratitude. I had on a natty white T-shirt and my favorite jeans. My hair was tufted. Pulling my sick leg like it was a ship's anchor, I yipped: "What's on, people!"

Rita was wedged behind the cash register. She graced me with a relieved smile. A smile that said sales had been nil that day. "The boys were worried about you. They thought you weren't going to show up."

Heller and 2-Time were positioned by the counter. Heller was sour. The first course of antibiotics had failed. Now he'd have to go back to the hospital. He leered at me.

"You ready to make that new prediction, kiddo?"

"No, I'm not."

I had inconveniently dropped an atom bomb. The emotional temperature in the room plunged ten degrees. For a moment, nobody said a thing. Heller spoke first, in delicate, polite sarcasm, frosted with a hostile smile.

"Come again?"

"I'm not doing it. Last time wasn't enough money."

"That's horse shit," 2-Time jumped in, riveting his bleary eyes on me. "We've already been through this malarkey. You got a fair share from the last job. If you want more paper, you've got to earn it. So far, you haven't. It's all your fault."

"2-Time's right," Heller needled me. "What we saw from you, that was amateur. Maybe you're just a hoax."

No tired ass old man was going to call me a hoax. And all the talking made the bullet twist inside my skull. It was like having an elephant step on my face. I paled and trembled. My sore leg palsied. The ringing in my ears went sonic.

The bullet counseled me, advising me not to sass 2-Time and Heller, no matter how disrespectful the fools were acting. It's all about the cash, the bullet said. Don't forget that.

I took a deep breath and exhaled. I felt my blood pressure drop. I had a swipe at the sweat on my brow and touched the scar. I looked at Heller, and didn't like what I saw. I hid my distaste behind a soft rumble.

"I'm no hoax. You hear?"

Sensing a compromise, Heller took advantage of it. He put his hands flat on the counter and grinned at me the same way piranhas smile when they see something good to eat.

"Show me."

I was at a dividing line. If I crossed that line several things would occur. One: I'd forget who I had been. Two: I'd turn into someone I didn't know. But since all of that was in motion—ever since I was shot—I opted for the unknown.

I had a twinge of foreboding, shrugged it off. I stuck a finger in my ear, wiggled it. The pain in my head receded into my nervous system. The relief was so great, I wanted to weep. Damn that bullet.

"Okay, I will. Let's do it now."

The tourist shop, aptly named Global Journeys, was a hundred yards west of Van Ness on Market. It had a chalkboard sign in the window advertising discount vacations to contamination-free countries in South America. Heller, 2-Time, and I had been watching the place for twenty minutes.

2-Time bitched at Heller. "Now what do we do?"

"Nothing. We wait."

"How come?"

"Because that's how it is, dumb ass."

In Heller's view, 2-Time asked too many questions. He was an interrogative machine. Annoying and useless. Heller snuck a glance at me. I slouched against a mailbox, the wind torturing my matted hair.

A stout, black-haired man in a brown Zegna suit and tasseled loafers, carrying two leather briefcases, approached the travel agency, opened the door, and went inside.

Heller motioned with his double chin. "That's the cat."

Five minutes later our quarry reemerged from the agency, bearing the same briefcases. Unaware that anyone was watching him, the bagman gamboled toward Van Ness, the cases slapping against his chubby legs.

Heller was shrill with excitement. "Ricky? Make the prediction. Does that dude have money?"

"Yup."

"How much?"

"I don't know."

"What do you mean, you don't know?"

"I predict events. I'm not a fucking accountant."

Heller was savagely disappointed. He thought my skills had a low ceiling.

"Okay, okay, but he's got a shit load of money, right?"

"Yeah."

That was all Heller needed to hear. Bonanza. Everyone knew a courier for the Honduran vaccine cartel always carried hundreds of thousands. But one thing disturbed him. Yours truly. My talents had limits. I was not television material, nor ready for Vegas.

"2-Time? Let's vamoose. You and me need to talk about this job."

Heller turned to say he was done with my services, but I was already out of earshot. I didn't want to know what he and 2-Time were going to do. It would be a travesty, and there was a limit to what I could stand. I moved toward Van Ness, to get away from them.

TWELVE

Hours after I made my prediction, Heller and 2-Time stationed themselves outside Global Journeys. It was a cloudless evening, roasting hot, reminding Heller that he should've worn something lighter, maybe a sweater instead of a coat, definitely not the goose down parka he had on.

"Get ready," he commanded 2-Time.

2-Time bridled at Heller's superior tone. Heller was continuously issuing directives—ever since he hooked up with that gold digger Mitzi and joined the 12-step program.

"Fuck, here he is."

The bagman strode down the sidewalk holding a briefcase in each hand. He paused in front of Global Journeys, craned his neck to see if the coast was clear. Satisfied that it was, he entered the shop.

Heller removed the Glock from his parka. He saw no homeless around him, which was odd, until he realized the hour—all the street people were at the soup kitchens in the Tenderloin.

"It's weird out here," 2-Time grumbled. "Too damn quiet."

Heller cast a scornful glance at 2-Time. He vowed if 2-Time didn't keep his cool, didn't keep a lid on his tensions, specifically his criticisms about Mitzi, harping on how she was undermining their friendship, always talking his sexist shit, he'd shoot him in the fucking neck.

The courier resurfaced from the travel shop, the street's lights in his eyes. Heller casually walked up to him and without any further ado, socked him in the right ear. The punch was hard enough to knock the guy off-balance, but not hard enough to make him drop the briefcases.

Heller shrieked at 2-Time. "Help me, asshole!"

2-Time's reflexes were lax. The bagman took advantage of his slowness and whacked him in the belly with the flat side of a briefcase. Doubling over, 2-Time capsized to the pavement.

The courier swung the other case and nailed Heller's cheek, scoring a bull's-eye on the cigarette burn. Heller never knew there was so much pain in the world. Blindly, he reached out and clamped a hand on a briefcase. He was close enough to see his adversary's clean shaven chin, close enough to smell the Chinese food that spiced his breath. The briefcase, like a child with divorcing parents, was between them.

It's ballet, thought Heller. So he kicked the courier in

the shins, causing him to yowl. Heller then pried the case from his grip. He backtracked and whooped, "Let's go, 2-Time!"

Dashing into the street, Heller was in front, the briefcase snug under his left arm. He sent a desperate, frantic message to his legs. Run fast. Outrun my enemies. Help me get rich. If you don't help, I'll fucking die.

Heller and 2-Time hurried down Market Street.

Nightfall descended with a guillotine's satisfying quickness. It found 2-Time and Heller tallying the loot in Heller's living room. Bundles of bills lay on the iridescent green shag carpeting.

"How much we got?"

"A hundred and nineteen grand."

Mitzi sashayed into the room, her breasts swaying counterclockwise under a thigh-length black rayon negligee, which was all she wore, other than a gold chain around her right ankle. Nonchalantly, she bent over a pile of hundreds and stroked it, pantomiming a hand job with the cash. Heller was mortified. Ignoring her, he carped at 2-Time. "How do we handle Bellamy?"

2-Time swallowed the lump of cynicism in his throat. Heller was bossy, mister big shot himself, but when it came to Bellamy, 2-Time had to supply the brains.

"Get your wife out of here so we can talk in private."

Mitzi overheard the comment. She didn't get Heller's friendship with 2-Time. 2-Time was quicksand, an inveterate asshole. Rita was no better, a classic codependent, sinking with 2-Time. Studying the money in her hand, as if she didn't know how it got there, Mitzi flung the paper at 2-Time. The wadded bills bounced off his red, veiny nose.

"Fuck you, chick! I swear!"

Heller watched helplessly as Mitzi fled into the kitchen and slammed the door behind her, depositing a trail of bitter vibes in her wake. Pretending he was indifferent, Heller confided in 2-Time. "Bellamy is not as capable as he thinks."

"Hell." 2-Time brushed money from his lap. "I know that."

"What should we do?"

"Give him his rightful share of the job."

"How much is that?"

"One thousand."

"A grand? He won't like it."

"Tough titty for him. If he wants more, he can predict another score. And we need the money. All we can get."

"What for?"

"To get the hell out of this town."

2-Time got up and walked to the window, opened black velour drapes stained with green threads of mold. He pressed his forehead to the cold glass and gazed outside. No cars were out there, no people. Nothing but a handful of epileptic streetlights flickering in the evening smog.

THIRTEEN

Rain hammered the club's roof well into Thursday afternoon. The main room was damp, mildewed, very unpleasant. Rita was stocking merchandise on the shelves. Heller, 2-Time, and I huddled at the counter. Heller explained why my cut was small.

"You fucked things up again. You predicted wrong. You overestimated how much cash the guy had. The job was a dud."

2-Time seconded the motion. "You fucked up."

He and Heller both thought I was a farce. I could foresee events, but not specific amounts of money. An oracle was supposed to predict anything, which I couldn't do.

I felt disconnected, as if I were staring through a glass wall at Heller and 2-Time. On their side of the wall was the money they owed me. On my side of the wall I was angry.

"How much you giving me?"

"A thousand bucks."

"That's low balling."

"No, it isn't. It's magnanimous."

I repressed the impulse to predict 2-Time and Heller's futures. It would serve them right, me knowing their fates before they did. It'd take their asses down a notch. But all I wanted was my money. The bullet would give me no rest until I got it. I stuck out my hand. "I'll take what I'm owed."

Heller slipped me a rancid manila envelope. I peeked inside. There it was, a thin sheaf of hundreds, old and smelly. The vaccine money stank of death. I crammed the envelope in my jeans, swiveled on my lame leg.

"Ricky?"

I pivoted toward Heller, to see what the fool wanted now. My scalp was tight, like I was on the verge of a prediction. I peered at Heller, and read right through him. If he had something to tell me, he'd better do it quickly.

"What do you want?"

"A prediction."

"You mean another robbery."

"Yeah."

"What's in it for me?"

"Plenty of money."

"You're a goddamn liar. There's been none of that so far."

"Because your skills are shoddy. But I'll give you one last chance to show me you're a real oracle."

My hair sagged, weighed down by the raindrops it had collected earlier in the afternoon. I was hungry and tired. I resented how Heller smiled at me. He reminded me of my dad, the time we went to an Elks Lodge dance, but didn't have the money to get in. Dad detoured us to a friend's house, somebody he knew from his first stint in prison. While mom and I waited in the living room, dad disappeared into a bedroom with his friend, got a blow job from him and twenty bucks for the dance. When he came out of the bedroom he had a phony, shit-eating smile, the same kind of smile Heller had.

I burred at Heller. "I don't give a fuck what you think." I spun around and propelled myself toward the door, my mind in a whirl.

"Ricky!"

Rita's syrupy voice, educated, full of books and college, stopped me cold. I looked at the door. I was five steps away from it. Shit, I thought. I cranked my head ninety degrees to the left and there she was, staring at me with the most vacant blue eyes I'd ever seen. I smelled the perfumed part in her hair. I felt bad for Rita. Marriage with 2-Time had to be a labyrinth.

"Where you going?"

I evaluated her question like it had global conse-quences. Aware that 2-Time and Heller were at the counter listening closely, I squared my shoulders and said with all the dignity I could muster: "I'm getting the hell out of here. Heller and 2-Time are disrespecting my shit."

"Don't listen to them."

"They're creeps."

"They envy you. You're a seer. A natural sage."

"I am? Thank you, baby."

"Will you work with us again?"

"No."

"Next time will be better. Please?"

"No."

"We'll give you a bigger cut."

"Nope."

"You won't do it?"

"No chance, girl. I'm sick and tired of being abused."

I made my way to the door. I eased into the street. A vicious wind was raping the rooftops. The rain fell in sheets, lashing the sidewalks. In seconds, I was soaked to the bone.

Across the road a homeless woman slept on the pavement, tucked against a Safeway supermarket parking lot wall. A pigeon stalked her, inspecting her hair, pecking at it, searching for food. Finding none, the bird flew off.

In hindsight I should've understood the chain of events that my defection from Eternal Gratitude would cause. I have only myself to blame for the things that took place thereafter. More telling, I wouldn't have been able to stop anything.

FOURTEEN

2-Time and Rita spent the remainder of the afternoon at Eternal Gratitude. 2-Time intuited Rita was upset about me and tried to soothe her. "Fuck Ricky. He was a figment of our imagination. A projection of our fantasies. He existed only because we wanted him to."

Rita couldn't look at 2-Time. The less money they had, the harder it was for her to be near him. "Ricky isn't genuine?"

"Oh, he is real, sugar, too damn real. He's a doppelgänger."

"What's that?"

"A mirror of you and me."

"I don't see him in my mirror."

"Don't be silly," 2-Time pooh-poohed. "Ricky was our hope to get rich. He fucked up and now that won't happen. The kid is handicapped. He doesn't have what it takes. He's too ghetto."

"Ricky was a competent oracle."

"The hell he was." 2-Time shook his head. "Ricky was low-rent with no vision."

"You guys treated him like dirt. He deserved better."

"Forget that. And we're fine without him."

2-Time's bluster sounded weak, even to himself. After Bellamy left Eternal Gratitude, he and Heller got into a tiff about how much angel dust 2-Time was using. Heller wanted him to join a harm reduction program. What a hoot. Heller could screw himself. The pious asshole.

If that wasn't enough, 2-Time had gotten a scary phone message from a friend saying the feds were planning to shut down all the Life clubs in the city. Before he could process what it meant, he also learned Tommy Doolan was on his case.

Doolan was the senior Department of Public Health official overseeing the city's clubs. Somehow, through the grapevine, he'd gotten drift of Heller and 2-Time's robberies. It was a bad scene. Doolan had the power to revoke Eternal Gratitude's license to operate. 2-Time was blue and said no more to Rita.

FIFTEEN

In my mind's eye I saw Heller was as tense as 2-Time. He was listening to the raindrops pinging against his living room's windows. His discomfort started when he and Mitzi went to lunch at a North Beach bistro. An old Italian place on Stockton Street. The waiter told them dairy items were off the menu, due to Fukushima-related contamination. Some vegetables like spinach were also too hot. Plus, he'd run out of potassium iodide, the over-the-counter anti-radiation tincture. Heller hated the tincture. It made his heart beat too fast.

As a bonus, Heller had the joy of receiving another telephone call from 2-Time. His partner was tripping, flying high on stress, kvetching that Tommy Doolan had him under a microscope and the Department of Public Health was going to investigate Eternal Gratitude.

The feds said the rainfall was safe, the regional contamination levels were insignificant. Nobody bought it. When it rained, the streets were deserted. Yesterday the newspaper said the rain contained iodine levels fifty times higher than normal. Since it was raining nearly every day, the radiation was accruing, similar to equity on a house.

Some people were already getting sick, struck down real fast. For most, years would pass before they even knew they were ill. That was the mystery of radiation sickness. You never could figure out when it would hit.

Mitzi waltzed into the room.

"Daddy?"

"I'm not your daddy. Stop calling me that. Jesus."

"Okay, okay, I'm sorry."

"What do you want?"

"Where is Ricky?"

"I'm afraid he's gone."

"Where to?"

"I don't know. Wherever failed oracles go. Bellamy is damaged goods, baby."

"Is he out there in the rain?"

"Probably."

"That's sad."

"It's his choice. Not my problem."

"I thought Ricky was your friend."

"Hardly. He was a business associate."

"You exploited him."

"I did not. He exploited himself."

"But Ricky is an orphan."

"Fuck that. He's a hustler."

The mess with 2-Time reminded Heller of the other

day at the Illinois Street beach. He'd seen three stingrays swimming in shoal water, gliding through it. The stingrays scattered ducks, sea gulls, cormorants, and pelicans, breaking the water's dimpled surface with their brown wingtips shining in the rain. Heller was certain the stingrays were an omen, a signal for him to move ahead with his plans.

Heller's share of the robberies was just under eighty grand. If he added 2-Time's split to the total, it was twice as much. One hundred and sixty thousand dollars. A sum that would lead to a better life.

Ever since Heller entered the 12-step program, he had his own ideas about making amends to the people he'd injured. Instead, he was more interested in getting payback from the dirtbags who'd hurt him. His list was long. It began with 2-Time. Robbing him tonight would be a celebration.

Heller didn't give me another thought.

SIXTEEN

I walked the length of Van Ness Avenue in the drizzle, past McDonald's, the old Jack Tar Hotel and the former Galaxy movie house, my kicks slapping against the wet pavement.

I was in despair. My budding career as an oracle was over. As Heller put it, my skills were shoddy. I didn't have the grit to be a seer. I was kaput. The bullet pleaded otherwise, begging me not to believe 2-Time and Heller. What did they know about the mysteries of the cosmos?

I was inconsolable.

When I reached Doyle Drive northbound traffic on the Golden Gate Bridge was slow. I followed the pedestrian walkway onto the bridge, trekked another hundred yards and halted. I peered at the bay. Only a few miles off, the lights of Berkeley and Oakland were invisible, lost in the fog. The wind had a snarl, truculent sea gulls blitzed the sky.

I thought about jumping off the bridge. Because there was

no room on this sad earth for an ass backwards oracle. No damn room at all. But jumping wasn't an option. Not yet.

Lost in my ruminations, I didn't see the two cops in yellow slickers creep up on me from behind. In a jiffy, they wrestled me to the ground. A Department of Public Health ambulance arrived and the cops plunked me in the back and cuffed me to a gurney. I lay still and pretended calmness while they interrogated me.

They wanted to know what I was doing on the bridge. I told them I was an oracle.

My answer led them to conclude I was suicidal. So now I was off to General Hospital's loony bin. In the nuthouse, I'd have to downplay my strange ways. While the ambulance rolled through the streets to the hospital, I did inventory, prioritizing which of my idiosyncrasies I'd have to keep under wraps.

At General Hospital I was booked and processed. I was tested again, and came up negative. My clothes were taken away, even my boxer shorts. I was issued an oft-laundered polyester gown and a pair of cardboard slippers. An orderly escorted me up a passageway studded with surveillance cameras to a cell that was furnished with a steel sink doubling as a toilet. A bed frame was welded to a wall. I dropped onto it.

I was starved and jittery, my blood sugar nosediving. I'd been processed so late in the day, I had missed the ward's afternoon meal and wouldn't get fed until later.

I flashed on the night Frank Blake shot me, how he

looked in the seconds before he pulled the trigger, his moussed blond hair, the tarnished silver hoop in his right ear, the cheap small caliber automatic pistol in his fist. I was asleep when the cell's door was unlocked and a burly, middle-aged doctor in a white smock breezed in.

"I'm Hess, your psychiatrist." He announced his name in a congratulatory tone, giving me the impression I'd won the jackpot. "Let's talk, boy."

I roused myself. It was a chat or a straitjacket. Hess squeezed onto the bed, deliberately crowding my space. He fired off an introductory salvo.

"You informed the cops you're an oracle."

"I did."

"Oracles were priests in ancient Greece. They made divine pronouncements. You're not an oracle."

"Who says?"

"I do. Are you suicidal?"

"Hell, no."

"The police said you were going to jump off the bridge."

"That's their opinion, not mine."

"Your medical records cite you were shot in the head."

"Yeah, I was. Last winter."

"You've been traumatized."

"True enough. I've been catching hell lately."

"Trauma lends itself to disassociation. The separation of the body from the mind."

I didn't take the bait. The separation I experienced wasn't between my body and mind. It was between my mind and spirit. My mind forced me to do things I detested, like working for Heller and 2-Time. My spirit wanted to be free of earthly concerns.

"My mind and body are together. After all the shit I've been through? Nothing can tear them apart."

"You need help. Medication is necessary. Your brain's chemistry needs readjustment. Anyone who claims to be an oracle is mentally ill."

I didn't care for that.

"Do you want to remain hospitalized?"

"No, man, I don't."

"Then admit you need help."

"Okay," I improvised. "I need help."

"Wonderful. I'm going to prescribe a mild dose of Haldol. An injection."

"Do you have to do this?"

"It's the first step. A big one. After the injection we won't put a seventy-two-hour hold on you. We're too overcrowded so you'll be released from custody. Just don't end up here again. Because next time, you'll stay. What do you say to that?"

Not understanding why, just knowing it was happening; the colors in the cell were bright and the air smelled keen, I augured the future, a tiny sliver of it. Next year Hess would divorce his wife, lose the house to her, pay huge alimony, and get in a car wreck. And because I wanted to get out of the fucking nuthouse more than anything in the world, I said what he wanted me to say.

"Thanks."

SEVENTEEN

An hour later the 48 Quintara bus thundered west on Twenty-fourth Street, jouncing by Galeria de la Raza, Sol y Luna Hair Salon, and Morena's Fashions before stopping at Capp Street. A drunk man in a smart gray suit boarded the coach and cut a path to the back, plopped into the seat next to me and began singing at the top of his lungs, launching into a bloodcurdling version of Michael Jackson's "Billie Jean" as the bus lumbered to Mission Street.

I struggled to prophesy his future, to find out if I could do it. My nerves twitched. I sweated. My bad leg had a spasm. I saw zilch. My powers, if I ever had any, were gone. The Haldol had done a number on me.

I changed buses at the next stop, climbed aboard a 14 Mission Express, took it to the Embarcadero and got off. From there, I did the Haldol shuffle to Mission Creek. I bumbled down a creekside footpath maybe twenty yards, saw a leopard shark with black and gold fins in the creek's shallows. The shark lifted its flat head out of the water and looked at me, making inter-species eye contact before abruptly submerging underwater.

It was a hell of a thing to see on Haldol.

Having no clear memory of how I got back to Guadalupe Terrace, though certain I'd had another seizure along the way, because now my left arm wasn't working for shit, I moseyed around the side of my house into the backyard.

Stuff left by the previous owner was stacked up by the fence. Lawn chairs, card tables with broken legs, a floor lamp, waterlogged photo albums and children's clothes, aluminum rice cookers, two of them, sneakers, high heels, galoshes, fishing rods, baseball bats, ping-pong paddles, prescription bottles, toothpaste tubes squeezed dry.

I knelt in the grass before the junk pile, unearthed a hand mirror from beneath a moldy bath rug. I held the glass up to my face, stared into it. A bellicose reflection glared back at me. Yellowed eyes. Slack, drooling mouth. Ashy skin. Scar redder than ever. Nobody I cared to meet.

I wanted to talk to God, but didn't know what to say.

"Ricky?"

I slowly rotated. It took forever, even longer. Barelegged and clad in a shiny black vinyl thigh-length dress, Spike was standing ten feet away from me. I coughed once to hide my shame.

"What's going on, girl?"

"You look like crap."

"Yeah, well, I had a hard day, you know."

"Where've you been?"

"I was, uh, at General Hospital. An emergency visit."

"What were you doing there?"

"I was in the loony bin. A little vacation."

"You were in lockdown? That why you look all fucked up?"

I silently conceded the obvious.

"They give you drugs?"

"Haldol. They shot it in my ass."

"Do you feel bad?"

"Completely. Worse than dead."

"What are you going to do?"

"Not much I can do."

"Why did they hurt you like that?"

"I scare people, I guess."

"You don't scare me. You're mellow."

Spike was extending a friendly vibe, but I couldn't navigate it. The chitchat exhausted me.

"I've got things to do. Sayonara."

I did a zombie walk to the cottage. The journey was eight yards. The Haldol turned it into ten miles. My legs were in revolt. Primarily my left leg, which categorically refused to cooperate with any suggestion I made. Each step was involuntary manslaughter. The rain was beating on my head faster than a drum machine. By the kitchen I made a half-assed attempt to boost myself through the window, but couldn't manage it.

I perched on the sill. Steadying myself, I searched my

pants for the grand Heller and 2-Time had laid on me. At least I still had that. I reached for the wad and cussed. Damn. It wasn't there. In slow motion I fumbled through all my pockets and came to a sodden, violent conclusion. Fuck. I'd lost the money.

EIGHTEEN

In Heller's unoccupied Woodward Street tenement cock-roaches ran amok. Joining the festivities, a band of houseflies circled the no-pest strips hanging from the ceiling. The land-line burbled four times. The answering machine erupted into a cheery salutation: "Hey, you've reached Rance and Mitzi. We can't take your call because we're evacuating from San Francisco and relocating to Mexico. No contamination down there. Leave a message after the beep."

The hysteria in 2-Time's voice was out of control.

"Rance? Are you there? Pick up the fucking phone. Listen, man. Eternal Gratitude was burgled. We were robbed. Can you believe it? Me and Rita were out get-ting some food and when we came back to the club all our money was gone. Rita is wigging. She says if Bellamy hadn't left us, this wouldn't have happened. I know it's bull-shit, but you try telling her that. Rance, I need to talk to you. I need your help. All right, buddy? I'm going to—"

The machine cut him off.

NINETEEN

Friday night I convened with Spike on her porch. I split a
tab of Life with her. It was late, past midnight. Moonlight
shellacked the leaves of the malnourished avocado tree in
the front yard. Each leaf was alone in the light, apart from
its mates. A shooting star, rarely seen over the city, arced
in the sky, passing too fast to make a wish on.

I shut my eyes and visualized the radioactive elements
that channeled through my blood. Cesium, plutonium,
and strontium. How I kept testing negative, I didn't
know. Spike held my left hand. Gently, not too tight.
Her palm was soft, fingers warm. I addressed her, unable
to sugarcoat the future.

"The cops are gonna come here soon."

"To do what?"

"Take back these houses."

"That's crap. Nobody wants this street. I'm safe out
here. And I need this place. Don't you?"

"Oracles don't have homes."

"Don't be an asshole. Everyone needs a home."

The wind was singing in the telephone lines. I smelled the exhaust from the cars on Geneva Avenue. I heard distant gunshots near Mission Street, peppering the spaces where there wasn't any wind or cars.

The Hondurans' bungalow was illuminated from within by hydro lamps leaking orange-white light into the street with the aplomb of a Halloween pumpkin. The rest of Guadalupe Terrace was scrolled in wearied blackness.

The bullet turned in my brain, something that had begun in the morning, indicating the Haldol was quickly wearing off. My oracular tendencies were resurgent, on the upswing.

Then Spike turned and kissed me. I didn't see that coming. It was the last thing I expected from anyone in the universe. I opened my mouth a tad and cemented my lips to hers, the kiss absolving me of the loneliness I'd felt since Vivian Raleigh. To her credit, Spike didn't complain about my insane breath.

The half tab of Life kicked in. My toes were numb, my sphincter was tight. Spike fluttered her hands, buzzed on the vaccine. "I'm seeing colors and patterns." In a few hours tomorrow would come like a woman telling a man their love affair was the best thing that'd ever happened to her.

TWENTY

Saturday dawned with a cap of reddish clouds topping the skyline. A northerly wind was gusting hard, stripping the sidewalk trees of their brown and gold leaves. I was broke and hungry. So I went back to Eternal Gratitude to rustle up some work.

My thoughts kept returning to Spike and the emotional architecture that connected us. Last night she argued the bullet in me was inhibiting my spiritual development, and I had to get it extracted. Like I told her before, it couldn't be done.

The icing on the cake was the typhoon that'd bashed the crippled Fukushima nuclear plant in Japan. More radioactive fallout had wafted over the Pacific Ocean to the West Coast. In the streets pedestrians now wore carbon filter face masks to protect themselves from air-borne contaminants.

I rang the club's bell. Seconds later, 2-Time's gaunt, lined visage floated up to the door, as if he were surfacing from the bottom of an aquarium. He wasn't surprised to see me and shot me a knowing, weary look.

"What the hell, Ricky. Why don't you come in? Everybody else is here."

Inside the club the sound of the rain pitter-pattered against the skylights. The house sound system played "Everyday People" by Sly & the Family Stone while 2-Time and I watched Tommy Doolan from the Department of Public Health inspect the premises. A thin man with a bad complexion, done up in a sherbet red suit from Macy's, Doolan walked the floor and stuck his nose into jars of Life. Thanks to 2-Time's misconduct, Eternal Gratitude was now under the Department of Public Health's jurisdiction.

Despite the downturn in his fortunes, a garrulous 2-Time was seemingly pleased to see me again and whispered in my ear. "Heller is a motherfucker. He came in here when me and Rita were gone and robbed us of every penny we had. Then I hear he's headed to Mexico. Him and that goddamn Mitzi."

After he finished checking the club, Doolan called a meeting. Without any formality, he notified everybody, meaning Rita, 2-Time, and me, that until further notice, 2-Time was no longer in charge of Eternal Gratitude.

Doolan then asked me what I was doing at the club. I said I was an unemployed oracle and needed a job.

2-Time lost his temper. "We already did that. You didn't cut the mustard. You refused to make more predictions. You walked out. You fucked off. You're passive-aggressive."

I'd learned to turn the other cheek when it came to 2-Time, but I couldn't do it often. Like now. "I know the future, asshole. You don't."

"I remember we had a conflict about the future." 2-Time's wry smile drew eloquent attention to the poetry of his missing teeth. "Because you were deficient. You any better at doing predictions?"

"I'm about the same."

"Ricky?" Doolan intervened. "Do you know what an intern is?"

"Someone who works for free."

"I'm offering you an internship with the Department of Public Health here at Eternal Gratitude."

"Doing what?"

"Making predictions about the contamination."

"What do I get out of it?"

"If you do well, you'll receive a wage."

"A wage?"

"Right."

"Not a salary?"

"No."

"Any commission? Percentages? Benefits?"

"No."

"Wages for an oracle?"

"Yes, but first, let's have a small test to see if you're for real."

"Go ahead."

"This is the test. Is there more contamination here from Fukushima than three months ago?"

I struck like a rattlesnake.

"Yeah, there is."

"That's the correct answer. You've got the job."

The job was sharecropping the future. I cleared my throat. "You've got to give me an advance. I need to eat."

Doolan shoveled in his pockets, dug around, produced four tattered bills, reluctantly handed them to me. I snatched the money and headed for the door.

I never got there.

The landline rang and 2-Time picked it up.

"Eternal Gratitude. Offering the best Life in the city. Quality products. Lowest prices. How can I help you?" His face darkened upon hearing who was on the line. "You've got your fucking nerve calling here, man. Who do you think you are?" He paused to listen. "I don't want to hear that shit. What are you saying, you did what was necessary? Only an evil bastard would pull a stunt like that." There was another pause. "You're here? Jesus Christ." 2-Time put the phone down. He looked at Rita. It was clear he'd received tragic news.

"That was Heller. He's back from Mexico. He wasn't even gone for two days. Something's wrong with him, and I don't want to know what it is."

TWENTY-ONE

I had grave forebodings about Heller's untimely return from Mexico. His troubles began when the Greyhound bus from San Diego lit into the downtown depot and he and Mitzi staggered off the coach, bags in hand.

Heller wasn't glad to be home. But it was better than Mexico. In Los Mochis he got the runs. The final straw was Mazatlan, when Mitzi said she was pregnant and wanted to come back to the city.

From the bus depot it was a quick taxi ride to their apartment with Mitzi keeping up a steady flow of pre-natal topics. "We're gonna have to get hazmat rain gear for me and the baby. I'm not going to eat any dairy products or leafy green vegetables while I'm pregnant. I won't eat local produce either. I don't want my breast milk con-taminated."

Heller had heard from 2-Time that Eternal Gratitude was on probation, courtesy of the Department of Public Health. 2-Time also said Bellamy was back at the club.

This didn't shock Heller. Where else would a tormented oracle find a gig? Maybe this time Bellamy would lead his flock to the promised land.

The taxi flew through the alley behind the welfare office on Otis Street, then to Woodward, pulling up in front of their building. Heller paid the driver, gathered his luggage and exited the cab. Standing on the sidewalk he looked at the moleskin gray sky, a lovely shade of gray.

Mitzi and Heller trundled upstairs to their flat. Heller unlocked the door, ushered his wife into the fusty apartment, wishing he had a Xanax. Mitzi puttered into the living room, flipped on the lights and caterwauled:

"Daddy!"

Mitzi was in the middle of the room, red-faced, fists clenched, besieged by overturned furniture and slashed black velour drapes. A message was elaborately spray painted on the walls:

FUCK YOU HELLER. I WANT MY MONEY.
2-TIME.

A song slipped into Heller's mind. Sugar Pie DeSanto's blues classic "Hello, San Francisco." Scissoring his arms around Mitzi's waist, he parked his chin on her head and listened to her heart thrum against his ribcage. He chanted in an off-key singsong melody, "It's all right, baby girl, it's all right."

"The fuck it is." Mitzi put her hands on his flabby chest

and pushed him into a side table. Heller reeled backward, windmilling his arms, falling to the floor with a thud. Mitzi towered over him, hissing, "Nothing's all right."

TWENTY-TWO

In the plaza at Mission and Sixteenth, beneath clusters of surveillance cameras and grimy palm trees, unlicensed Life dealers mingled with their customers, handing off tabs and palming bills. Life in the streets was unregulated, poorly manufactured, and full of toxic side effects, unnamed staph infections no antibiotic could kill.

Fog churned down the eastern slope of Corona Heights as I doubled back to Eternal Gratitude. A young, masked, bearded military veteran was sitting cross-legged on the sidewalk with a cardboard placard that read:

FALLUJAH 2006–2007.

Tourists walked around him, making like he wasn't there. I had ten bucks left from Doolan's advance. I laid five on the vet.

I still couldn't predict my own future. I suspected it didn't exist. Yet everything had a future. Animals and

insects. Buildings and cars. Palm trees and rain clouds.
Why not me?

I minced into the club, adjusting my eyes to the gloom,
spying Rita at the counter, noting 2-Time wasn't at the
door. There were no customers either.

"Hey, where's Doolan?"

Two red spots of disgust blazed on Rita's cheeks. "The
jerk set up an office for himself in the chill out room. He's
fucking up our scene."

Rita was right. The Department of Public Health's
presence at Eternal Gratitude would undermine the
club's credibility with customers. I backed away from the
counter, my legs struggling to work together. I wobbled
to the chill out room and opened the door. Doolan was
moored behind a steel desk. On the floor was a newspaper. The headlines were in big black letters. Contaminated seawater from Fukushima was crossing the ocean.
It would reach San Francisco in approximately twelve to
eighteen days.

2-Time said Doolan had third stage radiation sickness.
He also said Doolan's doctor gave him a year to live. How
you learned to cope with your death was sometimes the
only thing that kept you human. That was one lesson I personally knew.

I saw Doolan's aura was cloudy white, dense with contamination. It smelled the same as cheap flea market per-
fume. It smelled so bad I had to bite my tongue.

A radio on a shelf above his desk was dialed into a talk

show. A listener called in wanting to know the last time anyone had seen a black man in the financial district. Another listener called up to say white folks didn't believe the city's black population was shrinking because they always saw black people in the streets. The next caller said everyone was in the streets because there were no jobs.

"I want to tell you something," Doolan started up on me. "You've got a bad reputation for being difficult. Just because you can predict shit, that doesn't make you special. How come you're not in college?"

"I was shot in the head."

"Is that an excuse?"

"No. It's just the way it is."

Doolan digested my philosophical input. "Me and you are going to Pacific Heights. My boss lives there. He needs your help."

Nobody went to the exclusive neighborhood of Pacific Heights, unless they wanted to get busted for vagrancy. It was the richest part of the city. I didn't like the sound of it. I didn't want to go somewhere I'd get arrested.

I was querulous, and I was hungry again. I'd been counting on something to eat at Eternal Gratitude. In the least, some coffee and doughnuts. 2-Time thrived on that shit. He always kept some around.

"I don't want to go."

"What's your fucking problem?"

"Nothing. I just don't feel like going anywhere, that's all."

"You can't be doing this."

Doolan was half dead. I knew he was thinking about what hospice he wanted to get into, because there was a lengthy waiting list for the good ones. Yet he had to fuck around with me, someone who'd been next to death. Oracles were fragile. We had to be handled with velvet gloves. We had to be finessed. We needed red carpet treatment.

"Let's get going, Ricky."

TWENTY-THREE

Divisadero Street was a corridor of gas stations, hipster bars, secondhand vintage clothing outlets, toy stores, produce markets, and tourist hostels. The street's median strip was ornamented with saplings, a sign the neighborhood was upgrading, becoming gentrified.

With a bony hand fused to his sedan's steering wheel, Doolan drove us past the barbecue joint at the corner of Grove Street. KPOO radio station. The Hearing and Speech Center. Mount Zion Medical Center. He applied pressure to the gas pedal as we slipped by the chichi boutiques on California Street and crossed tree-lined Sacramento Street. The houses thereabouts were a potpourri of Tudors, Victorians, and Frank Gehry facsimiles. All the driveways had BMW sedans or Land Rovers, the ones that weren't in garages bigger than most people's apartments.

I hadn't said a word since we'd left Eternal Gratitude. I was still waiting for something to eat, feet propped on the dashboard, tapping my hands against my legs.

"Tommy? How come 2-Time and Rita aren't with us?"

"They're losers. They won't fit in."

"But I will?"

"You might be nobody, but you're an oracle."

He was buttering me up, fattening me for the kill.

At the top of the hill he executed a left-hand turn onto Broadway. From my window I had a glimpse of Alcatraz Island, the shores of Marin County, and the San Francisco Bay. The water was pimpled with whitecaps. The sky ebony black and unhappily marred with rain clouds.

Doolan turned right into a cul-de-sac and cut the engine. The sedan died in front of an orange stucco mansion with turrets and dormer windows. A vast, neglected lawn surrounded by a brick wall covered in red and white bougainvillea faced the street. A security camera semi-hidden in the bougainvillea winked at Doolan and me.

"We're here, Ricky."

No way was I getting out of the car.

"That's nice. I'll just wait outside for you."

"Fuck it." Doolan sucked in a deep breath. He had enough radiation in his body to fuel a power plant. "I brought you along for a reason."

"Why so?"

"You might know something about the contamination that nobody else does."

TWENTY-FOUR

A slight hunchbacked white man in a single-breasted blue Marc Jacobs suit, yellow silk shirt, and John Lobb shoes accosted me and Doolan at the mansion's lacquered black wrought iron gate.

"Tommy! Is that the oracle with you?"

"Sure is. Ricky? This is Branch. My boss."

I squinted at our host. Branch had a boxer's nose, broad nostrils flanked by scar tissue, dyed jet black hair combed off an aggressive forehead, a brow that jutted over hebephrenic brown eyes. He was somewhere in the no man's land between his late fifties and early seventies.

In turn, Branch measured me, absorbing my fraying jeans, unwashed since last week, the T-shirt ballooning to my thighs, the scar on my face.

He didn't offer to shake my hand.

Branch escorted us through a foyer and up a carpeted hall. Music gurgled in the background, soft piano jazz, tasteful, Mose Allison. Nobody else was in the house. I got the feeling Branch lived alone; he excreted loneliness, all dressed up with no one around. He shepherded Doolan and me into an office with a north-facing glass wall that commanded a view of the Golden Gate Bridge and Marin's bald hills.

I flung myself into the first available chair, the leather cushion squeaking under my ass. My stomach growled with renewed determination. I was weak from hunger.

"Ricky, did Tommy tell you why you are here?"

"Not really."

"Tommy says you're a seer."

"I am."

"Very good. He also says I can trust you because you've never been wrong. Since I value Tommy's judgment, I'm going to take a chance on you. You see, I'm the Department of Public Health's liaison with all the big businesses in town. My job is to make sure they stay happy in San Francisco. But since the Fukushima disaster and the contamination, things are getting iffy. And there's gonna be a mayoral election in a few days."

"So?"

"There are two candidates. The polls say they're running neck to neck. Naturally, I want my candidate to win. The guy who downplays the contamination. Because that's the only way major industry is going to stay here. This is where you come in."

"Me?"

"You."

I was in a swoon. "Why?"

"For new tactics. To give our side the edge. You can predict the future. You know if things are going to get worse."

The city had two realities. The first was a booming economic climate where everyone denied the contamination's impact. In the second reality, now unfolding, more and more people wore filter masks, inspired by the Department of Public Health's advertisements, which could be seen on Muni buses.

I assessed Branch's proposal. Let's say I predicted the right candidate. I'd earn a rep as a troubleshooting oracle. I might start a consultancy firm. Get some high class clients. If I failed? Too much paper was riding on what Branch was saying. I couldn't afford to fail. This wasn't Heller and 2-Time's amateur hour. It was a game where the stakes ran into the billions. It was enough to give me a teenage heart attack.

"I understand a vigilante shot you."

"That he did. It's a fact. You can look it up in the library."

"What do you know about him?"

"His name is Frank Blake and he's a chump."

"He should've been prosecuted for what he did to you."

"Yeah, right. Any moment now."

"What's with the sarcasm?"

"People like him don't go to jail."

I didn't want to talk about Frank Blake. He was off-limits. The one person I was willing to discuss him with was myself. Not Branch. Not the cops. Not Dr. Hess in General Hospital. Nobody but me and the bullet. The bullet described Frank Blake's hands as small with stubby fingers; the hands that'd pointed a gun at my face in a moment I don't want to remember.

Branch spoke above the uproar in my head.

"Are you healthy now?"

"I'm great. Real perky."

"You'll be handsomely paid for the prediction."

"That's cool by me."

"But we have a problem here. A pretty big one."

"Already? What the hell are you talking about?"

"Your clothing."

"Wait a minute, man, don't get weird on me. I'm wearing the best shit I got."

"Tough. Working for me, you'll have to dress better. I can't have you looking crappy, not in Pacific Heights." Branch wrapped up our conversation. "The next time we get together? I'll have information on the candidates. Statistics. Demographics. Spread sheets. Photographs. To help you make an accurate foretelling. I'll tell Tommy where we'll meet next."

I gaped at him. Help? A prediction wasn't algebra. It was a spiritual crapshoot. And him hassling me about my clothes? In my book, that was violence.

At the front door Branch said good-bye to us. He pointed to the adjacent mansion, an abandoned four-story Tudor with a gabled roof. A crude banner hung from the second-floor balcony. The banner screamed BLACK RAIN KILLS.

In Doolan's car I entertained severe doubts about meeting Branch. Predicting the next mayor? That was uptown, too rich for my blood. I lowered the passenger side window and let raindrops tickle my face. I was still hungry. Doolan turned over the engine, shifted into drive. His sedan boated downhill to Divisadero Street's flatlands.

TWENTY-FIVE

The second tête-à-tête between me and Branch—without Doolan—was five hours later at Le Central on Bush Street, a French bistro with considerable political history. Our booking was scheduled for six. At six-fifteen I trudged into the eatery. Large windows faced the sidewalk, booths and tables were tucked into the right wall, a bar ran parallel to the left wall. I was greeted by the maître d'.

"May I help you, sir?"

"I'm Ricky Bellamy. Here to meet Branch."

The maître d' consulted his schedule book, riffed through a few pages.

"This way, please."

I followed him past a row of tables. The people sitting at them were dressed up. At the bar every stool was occupied by someone in a suit. This was as close as I'd ever gotten to the financial district.

The maître d' seated me at a table for two.

"Mr. Branch will be here shortly."

A minute later Branch appeared. He was resplendent in a chocolate-colored Gucci outfit. He said hello to the maître d', then to four women at a table. He was smiling at everybody. He slipped into the chair opposite me, dumped a package and a calfskin briefcase on the tabletop.

"Good to see you, Ricky."

Branch signaled the waiter, scored two menus. He handed me one. "Get what you want. Dinner is on me."

That was white of him. I read the menu, couldn't understand half of it. All that French. I was also reading it upside down. Branch pointed this out to me. Eventually, I was ready to order. Flank steak and a salad. The waiter took our orders. I sat back in my seat while Branch quizzed me.

"You know anything about this place?"

"No."

"Then let me tell you. See that table by the front window? That's where Herb Caen used to sit. The newspaper columnist. The most famous man in the city."

I had never heard of him, but thought it best to keep my ignorance to myself.

"Le Central is where business gets done in this town." Branch leaned forward, his smooth face dead serious, no smile now. "You want something from city hall?" He rapped his knuckles on the table, jangling the carefully arranged silverware. "You come here first."

The bullet in me tightened. A warning signal I was

overstimulated. Before I could defuse myself, Branch pushed the package across the table.

"I got you something. Open it up."

I unwrapped the ribbons around the rectangular box. I lifted its lid and found myself staring at a polar white cashmere Zegna overcoat with a fur collar. I'd never seen anything like it. The damn thing was a magic cape. I pulled it from the box and tried it on while sitting in the chair, the rustle of silk in my ears. The coat fit me tighter than a condom. I was mightily pleased by its snugness.

"You like it?"

"It's super."

"Now you're dressed for Pacific Heights."

I traced a finger over the cashmere's satiny finish. I was humbled by its elegant smoothness. That coat meant more to me than anything. More than money. More than Life. Right there, I made a vow to myself. I pledged to never take off the Zegna. I'd wear it night and day until I died. Even after that.

The food arrived and we dug in. Branch demolished a platter of linguini pasta. He washed it down with an extra-dry martini. I gnawed on my steak, but couldn't finish it. My stomach was too small. The less you ate, the less you wanted to eat. The salad was unique, too. It had hard-boiled eggs in it.

Branch unpacked his briefcase and pulled out a pair of eight by twelve full-color photographs. Two pictures of men in suits. A white guy and a biracial dude. The white guy was leathery and bald with watery blue eyes. The other man was considerably younger, fronting a lavish toupee.

"These are the candidates." Branch spread the photos over the tablecloth like he was dealing me a hand of winning cards. "Babe Jones is a fourth generation San Franciscan and a hardware store owner from West Portal. He represents the Irish and Italian blue collar constituencies in the city. The other guy is Ronnie Shmalker, a physician in the Haight-Ashbury. He's my man. All the big money in town is behind him. I want you to take a good look at their pictures. Just study them. That's all we're doing here, getting acquainted with the subjects."

I devoted my energies to the photographs. First, Shmalker, then Jones. Shmalker had the magnetism of a cutthroat. Jones emanated mulishness.

"I don't know."

"You don't know what?"

Branch's vibes were negative. I hesitated. Some vibrations obstructed reception, got in the way of a prediction. Worse, were the pictures. I derived no feeling from them. No emotions or coloration whatsoever.

"I can't say who the winner is."

"First impressions are meaningful. What do you see?"

I heard the malice bugging beneath Branch's comment. When a cop with a gun threatened you, that was one thing. A man in a Gucci suit? He breathed and you started to sweat. I looked at the photos again as the busboy cleared the table, which broke up my train of thought. That's when I knew the Hondurans would hunt down 2-Time and Heller. Woe to them.

"It's gonna take time, Branch."

"We don't have time. That's why I hired you."

"Yeah, but these pictures don't tell me shit."

"Don't give me that voodoo."

"It's not voodoo, fool. These guys are the same."

"You're wrong." Branch stowed the photographs in his briefcase. "Dead wrong. Ronnie Shmalker will tell the public the contamination isn't a problem. Babe Jones won't do that. The asshole."

"So now what?"

"I don't mean to make you feel bad, but I have money. You don't. I'm a rich man. I'm more successful than you. If I say you're wrong, you can believe it." Branch rocked back and forth in his chair, having an autistic episode at my expense. "I'll see you at my house tomorrow. We'll talk more then. In the meantime, get prepared."

How can I get him to understand? Predictions happened, or they didn't. You couldn't prepare for them. You didn't organize them. You didn't corral them. They just blew up in your fucking face and you grappled with the outcome. That was the formula.

"Sure thing, Branch."

TWENTY-SIX

Rita was in Eternal Gratitude's doorway, observing a black man in a motorized wheelchair peel up the sidewalk, a boom box in his lap belting out James Brown's "Night Train." She reached under her dress and plucked at a bra strap cutting into her collarbone.

It was a calm Sunday afternoon. No rain had fallen. The sun even made a cameo, before getting sandwiched in clouds. The morning had been another story. 2-Time fielded several calls from Life club owners. One in the Mission, two others in the Sunset district. All were victims of overnight raids by the feds—a prohibition was coming down the pipeline.

2-Time decided to get ready for it. In a quick deal he copped a thousand tabs of Life from a Tenderloin wholesaler. A guy with a manufacturing lab at Turk and Jones. But the batch was cut with strychnine, 2-Time vomiting five minutes after downing a tab. Now he'd just gotten off the phone with Heller.

"Heller got the shit kicked out of him. He was way-laid by the Honduran street dealer me and him robbed. Heller was coming out of the liquor store at Fourteenth and Valencia when the Honduran shanghaied him back to the Woodward Street apartment and stole all the money. Then he broke Heller's legs with a baseball bat. Fucking hell."

The message was explicit.

The Honduran would be coming after 2-Time, too.

Rita hugged herself and retreated inside the club.

From where I was standing near the chill out room, I watched her stalk to the counter, her high heels clacking on the floorboards. She cut her eyes in my direction, quietly projecting an agenda I didn't want to touch. Heller, 2-Time, and the feds. Unremarkably, she said nothing about my new coat. To distract myself, I looked at the clock.

It was time to meet up with Branch again.

I dread the prospect. Branch is massaging me with threats, insinuations, demands, and generosity. He's invading me.

TWENTY-SEVEN

"What do you know about economics, Ricky?"

Branch, Doolan, and I were in a back room at the mansion, an enclosed glass-walled porch. Poised on the edge of a purple leather settee, Branch was in a mauve Brioni suit, silk ascot, suede loafers, his gelled hair massed like a storm cloud above his forehead. A tic worked overtime on his jawline.

I was stone-faced, camping on a plush couch, my kicks tracking dirt into the two-ply merino wool carpet. My cashmere coat was liberally spattered with mud from the street. I was miserable about that. Good clothes were high maintenance, really stressful.

"Not a whole lot."

"This is an era of permanent scarcity," Branch dithered on. "But nowadays there are new markets on the Pacific Rim. Beijing. Singapore. Hong Kong. Seoul. Vancouver. How long they'll last, nobody knows, because the contamination in San Francisco is putting a jinx on things. We need to fix that."

"What's that got to do with me?"

"The mayoral race. Ronnie Shmalker has to win."

"What if it's the other guy?"

Branch let his eyes do the talking. He didn't want my best prediction. He wanted one tailor-made, something like his suit. The bullet said: set this jive ass sucker straight. All the money in the universe couldn't buy the future. It was free. Whether you wanted it or not.

"It doesn't work like that, Branch."

"What doesn't?"

"Predictions. What if I told you economics has nothing to do with the truth."

"Shut your mouth. I'm not paying you for the damn truth."

"So when do I get some paper?"

"When you make the right prediction."

"The one you want."

"You got it. Ricky? What race are you? I can't tell."

"My dad was white and I don't know what my mom was."

"What does that make you?"

"I'm whatever the fuck you want me to be."

Doolan was beached on a velveteen divan in the room's far corner, partly listening to Branch and me, paying closer attention to the radiation infection tunneling in his gorge. The morphine he was taking for it didn't even dent the pain. On top of that, he'd heard Heller had gotten kneecapped by the Honduran dealer. It was only a matter of time before 2-Time got his. Doolan wanted to be somewhere else when that happened. He had enough on his hands chaperoning me.

I wonder if Doolan forgives the contamination for killing him. Can I forgive Frank Blake for shooting me? My left leg is lame. You tell my leg about forgiveness, and it will tell you to kiss off. I'm dirty in cashmere. When the day ends, I'll be down the hill at Eternal Gratitude. Don't talk to me about forgiveness, not now.

TWENTY-EIGHT

The last and most important debate between the mayoral candidates was held that night in the auditorium at Horace Mann Middle School in the Mission district. An overflow audience of roughly eight hundred people was in attendance, mostly working-class Mexicans and Salvadorenos from the barrio. The two candidates were seated onstage. Ronnie Shmalker was slicked up in a spiffy blue sharkskin suit, red tie, white shirt. Babe Jones was dressed in a gray polyester leisure ensemble, yellow bow tie, and brown oxfords, his bald pate shining under the overhead lights. The moderator, a young black woman from KQED television, was in a floor-length caftan, her hair molded into a chignon bob.

Branch and I had front row seats.

The debate jumped off when the moderator put Babe Jones on the spot. "According to statistics, the contamination from Fukushima is still here. What do you intend to do about this issue? And what is your stance on the Life clubs?"

He mopped his forehead with a starched handkerchief before answering: "We can't do anything, other than supporting charities and nonprofit organizations. We just don't have the resources. It's a job for the feds. But the cuts to the CDC and NIH budgets don't help any. And Life clubs generate revenue for the city. I don't see no problem with them nohow."

Ronnie Shmalker was right behind him. "I agree with my opponent. The fallout from Fukushima is a concern for our representatives in Washington DC. On a local level? There's nothing to worry about. The contamination is negligible. But the Life clubs need to operate under strict federal guidelines. Personally, I think they should be banned."

I slumped in my chair, dismayed by the candidates and their attitudes. Branch misinterpreted my posture.

"Got a prediction yet?"

"No. Those dudes aren't saying jack."

"They're not supposed to. This is just a friendly meet and greet session."

"That's uncool."

"You sound like a fucking Boy Scout." He extended his right arm, lassoed my neck and squeezed it. "I don't want to hear your shit. All I want is the winner."

"What if I don't know?"

"You'd better find out."

During the intermission I stood off to the side in the auditorium, near the restrooms. People milled in the lobby, talking heatedly about the candidates, nothing that I could get a handle on. Blips of conversation and forced laughter echoed against the walls, the din notching the ringing in my ears.

I was fretting as a young blond woman in a green silk dress came over to me. An unripe lesion glistened on her pert nose. She lightly touched my arm, establishing a tactile beachhead.

"I'm Ruth Dick. An aide to Babe Jones."

I blinked. The carbon filter mask dangling from her neck was decorated with rhinestones.

"I've heard a lot about you, Ricky."

"Who from?"

"Everybody. Doolan posted the results of the test he did with you. It's on his Fukushima blog. He gets thousands of hits daily. You're an oracle. The coolest thing around."

The flattering remark kindled my paranoia and speeded up my heartbeat. I tried to make like I was indifferent. In my job you couldn't act too eager, otherwise people would drain you until you were a husk.

"I have a proposition for you."

I hoped it wasn't sex. Please. I couldn't deal with that. The timing wasn't good. I was distracted. My hair was poorly combed.

"What is it?"

"Don't you know? We want you to work with our campaign. We'll pay you three times whatever Branch is paying you. Babe Jones would welcome an oracle on his team."

If I jumped ship, Branch would crucify me. The worrisome thing was, I couldn't predict the winner yet. Something blocked me. The auditorium crawled with too many vibes. It was too soon.

So this is politics, I thought.

I was nostalgic for Heller and 2-Time.

"What the fuck is going on here?"

Branch was at my side, devouring Ruth Dick with unconcealed venom, staring at her like she was a short eyes, a child molester. The tic on his jaw had blossomed into a twitch that ruled the right side of his face from his brow to his chin. He couldn't stop blinking.

"I was talking to the woman, Branch. That's all."

Ruth Dick attempted to speak out of turn.

"I had no idea you'd get so upset, Branch. I apologize—"

"Shut the fuck up." Branch silenced her with an imperial flick of his left hand, three gold bracelets tinkling on his wrist. His oiled black hair was electric with anger. "You're a goddamn leech. Get the hell out of here."

Managing to retain her composure, the campaign worker politely smiled at Branch, spun on her high heels and beat a judicious, swift retreat, merging with the crowd.

"If I ever see you talking to one of my competitors again, you're fired." Branch fastened his right hand around my forearm. "Do you read me?"

"Like the Bible."

"Good. Now let's get back to work."

The rest of the debate told me nothing. It was a stalemate. The picture was opaque. The sole thing I could predict was no prediction. When the event was over and the crowd filed out of the auditorium onto Twenty-third Street, Branch interrogated me on the sidewalk, holding me hostage against a parking meter.

"You come up with anything?"

"No, man, I haven't."

"We're running out of time. Each day is thousands of dollars going nowhere. You need to step up the pace, or we're fucking dead."

It was a warm San Franciscan night. Faces came out of the dark. Fog pillowed the rooftops, muting the streetlights. The air was thick with car exhaust, the ocean's salt and incandescent particles of iodine. Branch and I parted ways. I caught a 14 Mission bus to Geneva Avenue. He hopped in a limousine back to Pacific Heights.

Instead of riding the bus all the way south to Geneva Avenue I had the driver drop me off by the Safeway. It was late. Nobody was out as I slunk to Tiffany Avenue.

Frank Blake's house was at the end of the street, a large two-story single family dwelling sheathed in white asbestos siding. The yard was paved over with concrete. All the windows were dark. To one side of the front door was a rusty mailbox. I tippytoed to the box and opened it a smidgen; a torrent of Indian restaurant circulars and Department of Public Health brochures cascaded around my shoes. A handprinted note was taped to the box's flap:

POSTMAN. DON'T LEAVE NO MORE MAIL
FOR FRANK BLAKE. HE'S DEAD.
HEPATITIS C GOT HIM.

A light blinked on in the house next door. A young half-dressed female appeared in an upstairs window. Bare breasted with tousled hair. Looking down at me. Looking much too much like Vivian Raleigh for my comfort.

I withdraw to the sidewalk. I start up Tiffany Avenue. I don't look back. For back there was the man who shot me. The girl who took my virginity. Ahead of me is an unlit section of Mission Street. I'm alone with snapshots of what I saw tonight, the lesion on Ruth Dick's nose, Branch's rented limousine with one hubcap missing. If I had any Life on me, I'd take it.

TWENTY-NINE

2-Time weaved through General Hospital, avoiding nurses, orderlies, and janitors. He turned the corner into the ICU ward and found the room he was searching for. The door was open and he popped inside.

The room was painted a stark lobotomy white. A west-facing window showed the hilly skyline from Twin Peaks to Ashbury Heights. In one corner a television was tuned in to a football game. Four male patients dozed in gurney beds.

2-Time creepy crawled to the last bed and stopped short.

Heller was snoring with his mouth agog, his right arm carelessly flung over his head. His legs were encased in heavy duty plaster casts, the cigarette burn on his face worse than ever. 2-Time bent forward to get a better look at him, whispering, "How long have I known you? All the way back to the 1990s. When you could rent an apartment for six hundred dollars a month. How many lines of angel dust did we do? It must've been thousands of rails. You could've put them in a single line and crossed the country from coast to coast. But our friendship is over. It didn't survive your treachery."

2-Time fell silent and put his elbows on the gurney's railing. If he tried to imagine the future like Ricky Bellamy did, it scared the shit out of him. Who wanted to know all the fuck ups that were going to happen? Not him. The one thing 2-Time could predict was the inevitability of the Honduran dealer coming after him to break his legs.

The television droned like a mosquito in heat. Tiny pinpricks of light from the faraway Castro district did a tarantella through the window. All quiet, the night felt less sleazy than it really was.

"You're an asshole, Heller," whispered 2-Time.

Even though he couldn't see the future, 2-Time understood my dilemma. I don't know how I endured seeing all of tomorrow's fuck ups. 2-Time said I was a doppelgänger? Everyone knew the doppelgänger always got his ass reamed. I had to accept that eventuality.

THE SECOND WEEK

THIRTY

I was in high spirits Monday evening.

The fundraiser for Ronnie Shmalker was a twenty-six-hundred-dollar-a-plate function at Branch's mansion. I appeared shortly after six-thirty. I was saluted at the front gate by a valet, a slim young Mexican cat in a black shirt, white tie, and red vest.

"Do you want me to park your car, sir?"

"I don't have a car."

I met a greeter, the next layer of social protocol. "Good evening, sir. Are you sure you're at the right event?"

I forked over the invitation Branch had given me. The greeter opened the gate, and I schlepped into the foyer. I pushed on through the well-heeled crowd, moved past a triptych of Francis Bacon paintings and made a beeline to the interior courtyard.

A full-service bar had been erected under a canopy. A mob of besuited whites and Asians were scoring martinis, highballs, and wine from two bartenders while the house speakers blasted Howard Tate's "Get It While You Can."

I looked for Branch, but didn't find him. I didn't see Doolan either. A rotund red-haired woman swaddled in a brocaded yellow Vera Wang gown broadsided me, her breath moistening my neck with a bouquet of cigarettes, wine, and curses. "I have to get away from this shit. It's so fucked."

"Who're you, lady?"

"Julie Scott. I manage Ronnie's goddamn campaign. And you're the little fuckhead Branch just hired."

Someone tapped me on the shoulder.

"Ricky! You came!"

I did a half turn and discovered Branch smiling at me. His smile downshifted into a sneer when he saw Julie Scott. Branch condemned her with a laugh colder than a refrigerator.

"You're plastered again."

"Fuck you, Branch. I don't care."

"I do. You're compromising Ronnie's public image."

"That's big talk for an ugly little man. I've been in your bathrooms. There's nothing in them except suppositories and Ativan. And now you've got yourself a two-bit oracle. Why didn't you just find an astrologer? It would've been cheaper."

"Fuck you, too, Julie. You need to be in AA."

Branch grabbed me by the arm and towed me into the heart of the crowd. We made a pit stop at a couch where he superficially introduced me to a white man in a white tuxedo. Apparently the dude had been secretary of state under Reagan. He had to be a hundred years old, but he dressed well. Everyone at this soiree was immaculately decked out, down to the expensive carbon filter masks around their necks. Not me. Even with my Zegna, I was a ragamuffin. I radiated impoverishment. I hated myself for that.

I nodded at everybody, my head throbbing from the varying brands of narcissism ricocheting around the house. Branch then guided me upstairs to his office on the second floor.

The office's lights were sultry. A youngish man in a too tight chartreuse Armani suit accenting his meager shoulders and burgeoning potbelly stood by himself at the window, moodily staring out at the Golden Gate Bridge, the freighters in the bay, the sky pink and swollen with udder shaped clouds. From behind I couldn't tell who he was.

"Ronnie!" Branch whistled at him. "Bellamy is here!"

Ronnie Shmalker wheeled about, his angular face bloodless and white with red rimmed brown eyes that'd trawled a sea of unsleeping nights. His eyes hated me. To him, I was a circus act. At best, an asshole. He proffered a nicotine-stained hand.

"Hello, kid. I've heard great things about you."

The bullet twitched in my skull.

His hand was still hanging in the air. I gave him skin, snapping off a brisk, upbeat handshake. But the moment didn't feel right. I was anxious. His aura wasn't victorious. I couldn't stop myself and before I knew it, I made a prediction. Ronnie Shmalker was not going to win the election.

Branch smelled my negativity.

"You okay, Ricky?"

"Yeah, dude, I'm good."

"Let's sit down. You'll feel even better."

After Branch got us situated in comfy leather chairs, he grilled me.

"Ronnie wants to know if he'll be the winner. Why don't you tell us?"

What could I say? If I told Branch the straight goods, I was dead. Flat out. Branch would blame me for the future, when no one person could be blamed for it. It was everyone's fault.

"I can't do it."

"You're not in the mood, is that it?"

"Yeah."

"When will you be ready?"

"Later."

"You sure of that?"

Telling a lie was hard. Speaking the truth was harder. The territory in between, the strip of the unknowable, that's where I was. Ronnie Shmalker looked at me. A strange vibe passed between us. A telepathy with no idiom. The viscous sweat stains darkening the armpits of his Armani said he was medicated on Life. I gazed back at him and didn't say a thing.

Our meeting was adjourned. Gossip filtered throughout the fundraiser. No prediction yet. Wherever I went, in the kitchen or living room, people eyed me. Somebody asked me for an autograph. I graciously declined the request.

A little after eight I made my exit. Branch ambushed me

in the foyer by the Francis Bacon paintings, self-portraits that made the artist seem otherworldly. Branch looked the same. Dried spittle flecked his lips. His white dress shirt was monopolized by a flamboyant red wine stain.

"When are you going to make a prediction?"

I inhaled his cologne and pulled away. In the background his guests were shouting to the sound of cocktail glasses breaking on the terra cotta floor. I wanted to clap my hands over my ears.

"I need money first."

Branch thought about this for a moment. But I'd left him with no other choice. "Then I'll see you at Le Central in an hour."

I traipsed outside, raucous laughter behind me. The greeter was still standing sentry by the gate. I looked upward; the low sky seemed to mock my somber mood as I walked past a row of double-parked limousines to the street.

Near the corner of Divisadero and Pacific I came across a lone poster on a telephone pole:

HOW CAN WE PROTECT OURSELVES FROM CONTAMINATION? THE ANSWER IS WITH POSITIVE ACTION. WHEN WE TAKE ACTION, HISTORY IS CHANGED. SO PROTECT YOURSELF. WEAR YOUR MASK. AVOID DAIRY PRODUCTS. WASH YOUR HANDS FREQUENTLY. TAKE REGULAR DOSES OF LIFE.
—Department of Public Health

November was never my favorite month. All those dying, mottled leaves. The wind heavy with airborne radioactive particulates. I don't have a mask. That doesn't stop me from limping toward Le Central and my money.

THIRTY-ONE

At the same moment I ducked out of Branch's mansion the Honduran dealer, a vato loco by the name of Roberto Morales, hurled 2-Time against the back wall of a motorcycle shop off Market Street and smashed his legs with an aluminum baseball bat. He whipped the stick against 2-Time's knees, the ground eagerly rushing upward to embrace 2-Time.

Gritting his teeth to keep from screaming, crazed by pain and an inch from unconsciousness, a kaleidoscope of images funneled through 2-Time's brain, beginning with the eviction notice the landlord served Rita to vacate Eternal Gratitude. The club was shutting down for good.

2-Time expected the eviction, but he was taken aback by the self-loathing it caused. Without the club, he was nothing. Self-hatred was his middle name. No money was his game.

Mitzi had left the city and Heller in an exodus to her parents' house in Daly City to have her baby. She was also divorcing Heller. Still in the hospital, he wasn't contesting it.

In a television interview Babe Jones reiterated his campaign's position about the contamination: "I'm not saying the fallout isn't here, but I'm not going to say it's a threat to the people of San Francisco. The issue is still coming together and we'll have to play it as it lays."

The ugliest tidbit was me. I had a gig in Pacific Heights. Selfishly climbing the ladder to fame and monetary gain, I'd forgotten my homeboy 2-Time.

Roberto Morales swung his bat again. The last thing 2-Time heard was a squad of parrots capering over Market Street, their lungs bursting with music. Then he heard nothing at all.

THIRTY-TWO

Le Central was relatively quiet and uncrowded, apart from the folks at the bar. Music was on the radio, Irma Thomas doing "Ruler of My Heart." I sat across from Branch in a corner booth, staring at a clean white tablecloth, wanting to get the meeting over with.

"You're getting three hundred dollars for the job."

"Three hundred, huh?"

"Do you have a problem with it?"

Branch's unvarnished antagonism forced the bullet to advise me, like it had so many times before, that when confronting a complete asshole in a business situation, stay loose.

"It isn't enough."

"Don't haggle with me. I gave you that Zegna. I was overly generous with you. Come up with a prediction."

"When?"

"Now."

Part of me wanted to tell the truth. Another part said, forget it. The biggest quandary was the money.

"Give me some cash first."

Branch inserted two fingers in his Gucci jacket, shook out an alligator skin wallet, extracted a trio of spanking new one hundred dollars bills and gave them to me. I stuffed the paper in my jeans.

"Now tell me the future, Ricky."

"You won't like it."

I braced my hands against the table's edge. This was it. Ground zero. The time had come. I couldn't waffle no more. I had to tell Branch something. Even if it was bad.

"Ronnie Shmalker isn't going to win."

"Say that again." There was a threat in his command, a challenge to defy him. "Indulge me."

"He isn't going to win."

Branch cupped his chin with his soft hands. In the bistro's light, his skin had the texture of an orange peel. He looked wistful. Quite bemused. Then his face changed gears, his mouth thinned into a poisonous slit.

"This is bad news. You fucked up."

I had played my cards with integrity. I'd allowed Branch to see the future. And now I was about to have my ass handed to me for it. I chuckled in outrage. Branch chuckled too, enjoying my anguish.

"You blew it, Ricky. You were supposed to tell me what I wanted."

"Bullshit. I didn't do anything wrong."

"Yes, you did. You predicted the wrong future."

In only two days my stature as an oracle had taken me

from Market Street to Pacific Heights. In the last two minutes the whole thing had gone to hell. But what else could've
happened? My rise had been too fast. I'd reached for honey,
and I got stung.

I pushed back my chair, stood upright, brushed the
lint off my rumpled cashmere coat.

"Kiss my ass, Branch. I'm out of here."

THIRTY-THREE

I knew my prediction would send Branch and Doolan into a tailspin. A shade after eleven on Tuesday night, Branch clicked off the television in his office. The Channel Seven news had declared Babe Jones the official winner in the San Francisco mayoral race, calling his victory unexpected collateral damage for the reigning digital oligarchies.

Branch dug up his phone, punched in eleven digits and waited a moment. "Tommy? You awake?" He listened. "I don't care how ill you are, you're not dying. I don't fucking believe it. I'm always out in the rain. It's no big thing. What?" He listened again. "You need to do something about Bellamy."

Doolan sat on a love seat in his minuscule rent-controlled Russian Hill condo drinking thimblefuls of liquid morphine in cranberry juice. Billy Boy Arnold's "I Wish You Would" was on satellite radio in the kitchen. Earlier that evening he'd discovered several lesions on his face. Tomorrow he'd have more lesions.

The contamination was spreading, colonizing his body, conquering his immune system. The oncologists at UCSF's Mission Bay campus said he needed chemo. They said he had a year? What a laugh. He wasn't going to make it to Thanksgiving.

He couldn't remember last when he'd slept with someone, but no one was going to throw him a fuck now, not even a mercy fuck, not with his lesions.

A news bulletin that afternoon claimed flotsam from the Fukushima nuclear power plant disaster was expected to wash up on San Francisco's coastline sooner than its previously anticipated arrival. And infant mortality rates in northern California had spiked since the meltdown.

"Branch, you wanted an oracle."

"Ricky was something new and innovative. Then I find out he's no better than a tarot card reader. What can you do about him?"

Doolan had a sip of cranberry juice. "Not a damn thing."

The other day he'd participated in a raid at Hyde and Turk in the Tenderloin. Doolan and two plainclothes cops took down an unlicensed Life dealer. During the fracas, for an instant, he thought the police officers were Karl Malden and Michael Douglas from the 1970s television show *The Streets of San Francisco*.

The sicker he became, drifting toward delirium, the more convinced he was that everything was a hallucination. The Fukushima meltdown never happened. 2-Time was an illusion. So was Branch. Rita and Eternal Gratitude didn't exist. Neither did I.

The good news was the slot opening up at the legendary Treat Street hospice. The place had a backyard garden with a fountain. A jacuzzi. They let you have daiquiris in the evening and cigarette smoking was permitted. Doolan was fifth on the waiting list.

He threw his telephone on the floor. Remote and disembodied, Branch kept talking. "Tommy, things are seriously messed up. I'm losing it." Billy Boy Arnold's song ended, followed by the percussion of gunfire, three scattered shots from the Tenderloin in the rain.

THIRTY-FOUR

At sundown on Wednesday a street cleaning crew from the Department of Public Works, two middle-aged black men and a Mexican woman, all in fluorescent green vests and white hardhats, removed broken tables and mattresses from the sidewalk on Guadalupe Terrace, clutter that'd garnished the pavement for months. Spike and I monitored the threesome from her porch. I was antsy. Wherever the DPW went, cops were never far behind.

The female DPW worker wended her way up the lane to Spike's house, entered the front yard and walked over to the porch's bottom step, stopped there, put her hands on her hips and looked hard at the black girl.

"This is an abandoned building."

"The hell it is." Spike was on her feet. "I live here. Get it?"

"It doesn't look like anybody lives here, chica."

The DPW lady tipped her hardhat and had a gander at me. "Hey, I know you." The corners of her eyes crinkled with delight. "You're that kid they've been talking about on television. You're that oracle, aren't you? I saw your picture in the newspaper. In the fashion section. You were at a party. Some mansion and shit. Will you help me?"

"With what?"

"A prediction."

"I can't do it. I'm not in the business anymore. I retired."

"Please, baby. I'll pay you good."

I calculated my net worth. The three hundred dollars Branch had given me was a pathetic memory. I was broke again. My recent notoriety had done zip to improve my income. Being an oracle was glorified sharecropping. It didn't put enough food in my belly and as everyone knew, an empty stomach tends to make even the most optimistic person rather cynical.

"I'll do it for twenty bucks. Nonrefundable."

The DPW worker handed me two gummy tens. I gave her my unblinking and undivided attention.

"What's the problem?"

"My husband is stepping out on me with this other broad. Is he going to keep doing that?"

The question made me feel reborn. Something akin to a vestal virgin. For the first time in my career as an oracle, here was a task worthy of my hype, a prediction that wasn't based on someone's desire for material gain. This was a matter of the soul.

"Let me think about it for a minute."

I closed my eyes. I held out my hands as if they were dowsing rods. I listened to the cars on Geneva Avenue. The BART trains going in and out of the Balboa Park station. A police helicopter sidewinding over Mount Davidson. The ubiquitous hum of the Hondurans' generator. I let the woman's vibrations drown me in a tidal pool of anger and self-pity, loneliness and melancholy, the million nights she'd been alone. I reopened my eyes.

"I have your answer. He's going to keep on doing it."

"I knew it. I just knew it." She let out a majestic sigh. "I want my money back."

"What the fuck for?"

"I don't like what you said."

Debilitated by my auguring, I broke out in a cold sweat. I dropped my hands, letting them slap against my thighs. My gift was a curse.

Branch had wanted to dominate the future. That put him in the same league as Julius Caesar, Napoleon, Richard Nixon, and James Brown. Now the DPW woman was coming on with the same vibe, albeit at a lower frequency. I wanted no part of that damn world. I crumpled the two tens in my hand and fired them at her feet.

"You can have your money."

That was it. I was done. I wasn't an oracle anymore. Fuck the future. It was a waste of time. I signaled Spike.

"I'm leaving."

I stumbled down the porch's rickety steps and limped across the dead grass to my cottage. The flies that'd been living off the garbage in the lane were disturbed by the DPW crew's clean up. They flitted everywhere. A bunch of them haloed my head, in love with my hair.

THIRTY-FIVE

I laid down on the kitchen floor and curled up inside my grimy cashmere overcoat. Manufacturing predictions was murdering me. With each one I made, I lost a slice of my spirit that would never return.

I'd had no vaccine in days because the drug was off the market—the feds shuttered all the clubs. I was having Life withdrawals. Cotton mouth. Hot and cold sweats. Spastic colon. Torrential diarrhea.

Spike told me debris from Fukushima was landing on Baker Beach, almost two miles south of the Golden Gate Bridge. The beach, traditionally employed for nude sunbathing, had been quarantined by Homeland Security until further notice.

I had a flashback about my mother before she died, the two of us in an empty room. I was walking on my tiptoes, doing it quieter than a cat burglar. Mom instructed me, "Keep practicing. You need to walk silently. That's how a poor man survives in this city."

Silent as a ghost.

Doubting that I'd ever wake up, not caring if I did or didn't, I drifted off to sleep, the whitened outline of Frank Blake rearing above me, his puffy hepatitis C face dancing in and out of focus. "I killed you once, Ricky. I can kill you again."

He was washed away by a wave of slumber before I could call him an asshole.

A stiff wind blew through the night on Guadalupe Terrace. A dog barked like someone had driven a stake in its heart. Then, the Hondurans' bungalow detonated into a fireball. The roof caved in and the windows buckled, followed by reeking clouds of burning vaccine chemicals.

I bolted to my feet, scurried to the kitchen window and stood still; the searing heat of an electrical fire scorched my nostrils. Zipping up my overcoat, I leapfrogged out the window and rounded the cottage to the driveway.

Three fire engine trucks and a police car were already parked by the bungalow, teams of firefighters were unwinding water hoses. The front wall crumbled, sucked into the fire's inhalation, forcing the firefighters to retreat.

I had a vision: the Hondurans were trapped inside. They were crouching in the laundry room, staying below the smoke.

The nearest cop noticed me, unholstered his service weapon and aimed the pistol at my nose. I looked at the muzzle of his chrome-plated .40 semiautomatic. The bullet in me thundered, don't let him shoot you.

"Halt right there, shithead."

"But I'm here to help."

"Yeah, sure. Now go fuck yourself."

How do I tell a cop I have a bullet in my head that shows me the ways of the world? How do I explain I was shot by a vigilante for no good reason? It was a twenty-first century disease. But I'd survived and now I could see things like nobody else. I was a cartographer of human souls.

"I'm Ricky Bellamy."

"The oracle?" The cop reholstered his weapon, turned to the chief firefighter and jerked a thumb at me. "This is that guy we've been hearing about."

"The weirdo that's been in the newspapers?"

I nodded.

"What're you doing here, kid?"

"I know how to save the people in there."

"You sure?"

How does a soothsayer explain he knows the truth? That he can perceive what is on the farthest side of darkness. That prophecy is a language which never errs.

"I'll bet my life on it."

"It isn't your life you'll be betting."

I judged the threat, decided I wasn't afraid. I put my mind to the task. I searched and searched the gloomiest corners of the spirit world until a sole image was fixed in my consciousness: the Hondurans.

"Follow me."

We scampered to the back of the burning bungalow with me in front, trumpeting: "They're in the laundry room. Break through the door to the kitchen and you'll find them."

The firemen hefted their axes, made short work of the door and disappeared into the flames. A tongue of fire ran up a nearby telephone pole.

Shaken by the divination's intensity, I was worried. What if I'd made an error? Those men would perish and I would go to prison. There, I'd fight to keep from getting raped. My dad never talked about it, but mom steadfastly maintained he'd been punked and turned out in the pen. Mired in my anxiety, I didn't hear the triumphant shouts rising above the fire's cruel roar. Three firefighters materialized from the smoke, pushing and shoving the two Hondurans toward safety.

"Fuck." One of the cops gawked at me. "You did it."

Without saying a word, I pirouetted on my heel and flounced down the street, the tatty Zegna coat hanging from my emaciated frame like the magic cape that it was. A hummingbird streaked past my shoulder, chased by five hypertensive crows. I glanced at Spike's place. I didn't see any sign of her.

Sunrise was an hour away. I wasn't looking forward to it. I was close to cracking up. The mental strain of this prediction had done me in. But there would be no respite for me. To the contrary. I was back in the saddle again. The days were going to move faster now. Hopefully, I wouldn't.

THIRTY-SIX

The news of my exploit had long legs. Saturday morning found me sitting in the basement of the Emergency Management Center on Turk Street. The building was a superstructure with a metallic exterior, tinted windows, and a swooping roof stippled by satellite dishes and transmission poles.

The basement boasted blue industrial carpeting, embedded ceiling lights, and beige walls, a sickly fifty-year-old white man in a lime green Brooks Brothers suit occupying the room's other chair. His fingernails were razed to the quick, the cuticles colored with blood. Frowning at his nails, he looked at me, still frowning, the runnels around his mouth deeper than a canyon.

"Ricky? I'm Bo Lackner. The director of the city's disaster containment unit. Thanks for coming. You've been highly recommended to us by the new mayor."

He was prematurely brown-nosing me. I curled my lip. "I didn't do fuck all for him."

"You predicted the defeat of his opponent. Your reputation is spreading. Everyone knows about your honesty
and unerring accuracy. As an oracle, do you make predictions from a need to do good for society?"

His question was spot on. When I started dispensing predictions for Heller and 2-Time, my motives were selfish. I
wanted money. I didn't understand the consequences of
my actions. My interaction with Branch and the circles he
traveled in, the corridors of power, allowed me to think in
larger terms. The fire on Guadalupe Terrace showed me I
had a responsibility to other people. That was part of my
accursed gift. I had become an agent for change. I wasn't a
politician. I wasn't a social worker. Those roles were pieces on
a chessboard. I was the chessboard itself. I wore the cloak of
prophecy. I no longer catered to the greed of men. I carried
the burdens of the city. I was on my way to Jerusalem.

"Yeah, I do. But do you know Branch?"

"Yes, everybody does."

"He wasn't pleased by the job I did for him."

"Forget him. He's finished."

"So what can I offer you?"

"We're facing a problem. All of us in Emergency Management are expecting more airborne contamination
from the Fukushima disaster to strike San Francisco. If
you predict when it will happen, lives can be saved."

It was hot in the room, but I refused to shed my coat.
The cashmere was a good luck charm, a talisman. It was a
smorgasbord of spoor, smoke, and my filthy skin.

"You're gonna give me a job?"

"That is my intention."

"To predict another wave of fallout?"

"Yes."

I didn't want to hear any more. The stress of the situation was already getting to me. Yet if I didn't take the job, life would be hell for other folks. "Tell me the details."

"More contamination will disrupt the city. Looting and shootings. Fires. Food shortages. The poorest neighborhoods, the Tenderloin and Hunters Point, will suffer the most. And since this is the most expensive city in the country to live in, with extra contamination, it will be even more expensive. For example, the cost of getting clean water will be prohibitive. A preemptive prediction can help everybody."

"I predict events, but I can't quantify things." I thought of 2-Time and Heller and their robberies. "I can't predict specific amounts of anything."

"But that's perfect. This is our credo: it's life after Andy Warhol. Everything is guaranteed fifteen minutes of anonymity and the rest is surveillance for eternity. All we want you to do is track the fallout's path."

I watched the air in the room. The rug under my feet smelled. I wasn't who I used to be, not even from a week ago. I didn't know who Andy Warhol was, either. Lackner crossed his legs, repositioned his balls, hiked a pant leg, giving me a candid shot of his hairless white ankle, an old man's ankle. I looked away before I got upset.

"Do I get a salary?"
"Of course."
"How much?"
"Four hundred a month."
"That's all?"
"We have a limited budget."
"Any medical benefits?"
"None."
"Why not?"
"You're being hired as an independent contractor, not as a permanent employee. You aren't eligible for benefits."
"This job, how long is it going to last?"
"A week."

Lackner was another version of Branch, yet with less finesse, demarcated by the quality of his clothing. But his attitude was on the same channel. I summed up the money in my pockets, a grand total of practically nothing. My head, tipsy from hunger, was lighter than a cloud at high altitude. My diarrhea was digging in its heels.

"I'll take the position. When do I start?"
"How about this afternoon?"
"I need to go to Oakland first."
"Why?"
"To get some anti-radiation tincture. It's all sold out here."
"Okay. When you return we'll start our research."

It occurred to me that I'd made a pact with a dybbuk.

But where was Jerusalem? It wasn't at Eternal Gratitude. It wasn't on Market Street. It wasn't in Pacific Heights.

Wherever it lay, loneliness was a thing of the past and 2-Time was in rehab. I longed for Jerusalem.

THIRTY-SEVEN

I rode the BART train back to San Francisco from Oakland, a Walgreens potassium iodide tincture vial secure in
my shirt pocket. In the city I got off at the Montgomery
Street station. I walked westerly on Market Street through
the hysteria of the noon hour crowds to the Emergency
Management Center. Trash minueted at the curb by Pip-
er's Jewelers, World of Stereo, and the Psychedelic Smoke
Shop. Feckless pigeons invaded my space, brushing past
my face with an arrogant flick of their wings, letting me
know they could take a dump on my head any time they
wanted to.

At the intersection of Seventh and Market, where
the Odd Fellows Temple, Travelers Liquors, Ho King
Grill and the old Strand movie house stood together,
the sidewalk was rich with junkies. Pedestrians eddied
around me, adrift in dread about their lives. The bill-
boards above their heads told them to buy life insur-
ance. The cement under their feet exuded melancholia,

the improbability of a viable future for themselves and their loved ones.

It was Eternal Gratitude's final day.

Rita had packed the triple-beam scales into a cardboard box cushioned with styrofoam peanuts. The bogus banner 2-Time had forged, naming the club as the best in the city, was in a garbage can by the counter. The phony Turkish carpets were neatly folded, ready for their journey to Goodwill. The sound system, the speakers, turntable, and amplifier, had been dismantled and stacked up at the door. The remaining Life stock, three jars containing one hundred tabs each, was in an iron strongbox. It was a low grade variety of the vaccine, virtually worthless on the market, the tainted strychnine batch 2-Time had purchased from the Tenderloin wholesaler.

2-Time himself was enthroned in a wheelchair and watching the Channel Two news on a portable television, live footage of the Fukushima debris streaming under the Golden Gate Bridge into the San Francisco Bay. The debris had unexpectedly coagulated into a solid mass off the coast near the Farallon Islands. Powered by offshore winds, it was migrating eastward to the Berkeley marina. A flotilla of Navy destroyers escorted it.

A close up of the radioactive waste showed car tires, refrigerator doors, plastic bottles, sinewy ropes of seaweed, water soaked boards, and birds sitting on splintered boat hulls.

The camera then panned to the panicking throngs on the beach at Aquatic Park a few blocks west of Fisherman's Wharf. Dozens of SWAT cops in riot gear were restraining them. The camera zoomed in: anguished faces contorted with horror filled the television screen. The cops waded into the crowd, herding people away from the beach and up the hill to Bay Street.

What a fucking mess, 2-Time thought.

THIRTY-EIGHT

By four o'clock Lackner and I were atop windswept Twin Peaks. Below us, the city stretched from the bay to the ocean. We could see everything from the piers at the Embarcadero to the shuttle buses in Golden Gate Park.

Lackner had given me his office files, radiation readings that'd been compiled over the last few months, but none of it meant more than an old phone book. I needed to be outdoors, to see the contamination.

"Take a look, Ricky, and make a prediction."

I worked myself into a trance and first looked at the Tenderloin. The soup kitchen line at St. Anthony's Dining Room was two blocks long and direct from a 1930s Dorothea Lange photograph. The sidewalks were congested with vendors selling books and clothes, hustlers pacing by the check-cashing store on Market. Up the street was the citadel-like Twitter headquarters.

I trained my powers on the Haight-Ashbury. Homeless crusty punks were powwowing in the Panhandle. They sat in a ring by the basketball courts, straight out of central casting from *Lord of the Flies*.

I focused my energies on the Mission. Salvadoreno cowboys in big hats promenaded down Clarion Alley. The regal New Mission movie house's marquee was an angel of grief backlit by the palm trees on Mission Street. Further away, UCSF's Mission Bay complex confronted the crosstown freeway overpass for supremacy of the sky.

"What do you say, Ricky?"

"Nothing good."

I did a one-eighty and took in the city's westside. The Bank of the Orient and Wu's Healing Center on Clement Street bustled with customers. The Great Highway teemed with traffic running south to Fort Funston and north to the Cliff House and the Golden Gate Bridge. Ocean Beach was drenched in Fukushima waste. I was done divining.

"I've got enough information."

"So what do you think?"

"It's bad."

I stuck my hands in my pockets as more rain flogged the backside of Twin Peaks, white fog lapping against the condos on Diamond Heights. Despite my cashmere coat, I was chilled. My kicks were totaled, heroically kept intact with duct tape.

"How bad?"

Heller said it best nearly two weeks ago at Eternal Gratitude: "Ricky, you should be on anti-depressants, some kind that has a sedating component to it. You're the most stressed out person I've ever met."

But I didn't need anti-depressants. What I needed was sleep. A hot meal. A reason to believe everything would be all right in a world beyond repair. Lackner believed I was in sync with his strategy. He was off-base. I decided to make him suffer for it.

"I'll tell you tomorrow, okay?"

"That's not acceptable. You're working for the city on the clock."

"Then dock me."

"But we need to know now."

"Fuck you, man. I'll talk when I'm ready."

I limped down the hill's slope to Crestline Drive, to where Lackner had parked his Ford Crown Victoria. Grudgingly, he followed. He opened the driver's door and got behind the wheel.

"I should make you walk."

I vaulted into the front passenger seat. He started the car, turned on the radio. The jazz strains of Pharoah Sanders's "You've Got to Have Freedom" heated our ears as dusk, solitude's favorite hour, curtained the city.

THIRTY-NINE

It was closing time on Sunday at the Emergency Management Center. Lackner was in his office, fighting off a migraine headache. Everything he'd done had a reason, not to increase his mastery over the city, but to make it safe from danger. And he was furious at me because I quibbled yesterday that I couldn't commit to a prediction. Moreover, he'd received a text message from one of my previous employers:

> LACKNER. YOU THINK RICKY BELLAMY CAN PREDICT RADIATION? DROUGHT? ECONOMIC COLLAPSE? WAR? AIRPLANE CRASH? NO, HE CAN'T. HE'S A LOSER. A ROGUE ORACLE. HE WILL FUCK YOU OVER. BRANCH.

I showed my ID card to the security guard at the front desk, then ghosted down a corridor to Lackner's windowless lair. I was two hours late for our summit conference. Two hours late for the answers I was supposed to deliver.

I toddled past cubicle after cubicle while organizing my thoughts. What I had seen on Twin Peaks terrified me.

I knocked on Lacker's door, went in. He was entrenched in an overstuffed chair. Quick as a match lit in a dark room and dying just as fast, I deduced he would have a coronary for Christmas.

A deduction was the stepchild to a prediction.

I said nothing of it.

Knowing that Lackner would have a coronary let me see him in a different light. His spirit was already preparing to depart from his body. But my job wasn't to tell a grown man he might be dead at Christmas, it was the safety of eight hundred thousand San Franciscans.

"You're tardy, Ricky. Take a seat."

"I don't want to."

"Suit yourself. Now let's have your prediction."

I perspired in my coat. The office's fluorescent lights sizzled. I was going to make a prognosis about time. That was queer. I was no clock.

"Okay. More contamination is coming day after tomorrow."

"That soon? How do you know?"

No oracle had to explain himself. The future wasn't a schoolbook read by the many. It was a mystery known to a few.

"I just know. When do I get a paycheck?"

"You don't get one. We do direct deposit."

"I don't have a bank account."

"Fuck your bank account. Where is the contamination going hit?"

"It'll pass over the Tenderloin."

I turned to leave.

"Ricky? How do I get ahold of you?"

I thought about the cottage on Guadalupe Terrace and larded my response with spite.

"You can't."

I stormed out of the Emergency Management Center and zagged over to nearby Jefferson Square. The park was empty, other than a parrot arguing with itself in a eucalyptus tree. I seated myself on a bench. Black rain wept against my Zegna. The prediction I'd told Lackner had taken all my energy. I had nothing inside myself, just a tundra of vacancy. No hope. No anticipation. Nothing but a fist of fear inside my chest trying to sock its way into my mouth.

I'd never prayed for anything before. But now I said a prayer for the Fukushima disaster survivors. I mumbled a prayer for the homeless Iraq War veterans on Market Street. I evoked a prayer for the assholes I abhorred, 2-Time, Heller, Branch, Doolan, and Lackner. Then I prayed I was wrong, that more fallout wouldn't hit the city. I remembered 2-Time saying, "You're a hostility magnet, Ricky. All the trouble you get into is because you're not only working out your own shit, but everything that's happening to the people around you, too."

I finished praying and left Jefferson Square.

I was gimping toward the projects on Laguna Street when I bumped into Vivian Raleigh. She still looked healthy. Obviously, she'd tested negative. She was tricked out in a paisley print rayon minidress and a full-length black leather trench coat, leading a terrier on a leash. The dog took one look at me and lunged for my pants. Vivian jiggled the leash and the terrier fell back.

She checked out my Zegna, aware of its costliness.

"That coat is fucking sad. Don't you know how to take care of your clothes? You're no better than a wino."

"Thanks."

"Didn't I see you the other night on Tiffany Avenue? I was at my boyfriend's place."

"It wasn't me."

The memory of how she took my virginity came to me in an unwanted rush. We'd been alone at a friend's house. I kissed her, tasting another guy's lips on her mouth, smelling his sweat on her skin. When we took off our clothes and I reached between her legs, my fingers discovered she was sticky with his seed. I wasn't the first man Vivian had fucked that day. We flopped to the floor with Vivian on top. She mounted me. No missionary position for her, no doggy style. Then, with a deft hand, she inserted me in her famished slit. Her breasts teased my nose, and her knees pinned my hips. I thrust upward once. Vivian pulled out as I ejaculated.

"It felt good, huh?" she crooned.

All I had to commemorate my first sexual joining with

another human being—lasting fifteen seconds—was a puddle of semen on my stomach. I wanted to kill myself.

Vivian dismounted me, somersaulted off the floor, retrieved her clothes and stepped into her panties. She stared at my face, reveling in her power. Another virgin had bitten the dust.

The memory faded and I rebounded back to the present. "Hey, girl." I smiled in pain. "It's good seeing you again."

I walked on.

Opposite St. Mary's Medical Center on Hayes Street a young man in gym shorts—a double amputee from his thighs down, a contamination survivor in physical therapy—sprinted up the sidewalk on black carbon steel prosthetic legs. His artificial feet, two curved stainless steel blades, boomed against the pavement.

I shouted, "Go, brother, go!"

Without breaking his stride, he huffed, "Mind your own damn business."

FORTY

On Tuesday at dawn air raid sirens blared from Noe Valley to Chinatown. Exercising his office's powers, Lackner had ordered the evacuation of the Tenderloin—with approval from the feds. The neighborhood was emptying with a steady line of vehicles snaking west on Lombard Street to the Golden Gate Bridge.

Among the evacuees were Rita and 2-Time. They were in the last row of the early morning Greyhound bus bound to Fort Bragg in Mendocino County. Unluckily, due to extreme traffic, the bus had been stuck on the bridge for an hour.

2-Time rearranged himself in his seat. He smoothed the *San Francisco Chronicle* newspaper in his lap. An article in the business section held his attention:

DEPARTMENT OF PUBLIC HEALTH OFFICIAL
ATTEMPTS SUICIDE.

The story reported Branch, despondent over recent financial setbacks, coupled with an inability to pay his mortgage, had overdosed on alcohol and cold tablets. He was in critical condition at General Hospital.

2-Time relaxed, ignoring the bus restroom's Lysol odor. His broken legs ached, but the pain was bearable, thanks to the river of Percocet in his bloodstream. He stared out a window. Coit Tower and the Bank of America building were stapled against the tan sky. Navy helicopters flew above Alcatraz Island. The Fukushima waste mass was serenely cruising toward Berkeley, a northwesterly wind molesting the incoming waste, plastic containers inscribed with Japanese script bobbing in the shoals.

2-Time pondered over recent events, assembling all the bits of hearsay that'd come his way since the previous day. Doolan had been found unconscious in his Russian Hill condo, his face blanketed with lesions. At a UCSF clinic surgeons performed an emergency tracheotomy on him and removed a malignant growth from his esophagus, but he'd died on the operating table.

Heller was recuperating in a convalescent home in Palm Springs near his retired parents. His used car lot had been left abandoned, in lieu of unpaid back taxes.

2-Time and Rita's landlord had taken possession of Eternal Gratitude and was leasing the property to Chinese investors who planned to revamp the space into a restaurant. Then the Honduran cartel that Heller and 2-Time had jacked put out a contract to snuff them. Then there was Bellamy. The big hero with a cushy job as an Emergency Management consultant.

"Hey, folks," the bus driver's voice crackled over the intercom, "traffic is slacking off. We're moving."

The Greyhound coach inched forward.

2-Time elbowed Rita, wanting company. "You know what I think?"

Drowsily, Rita turned in her seat to face him. "What's that?" She wanted to sleep for a thousand years. But it wasn't possible with 2-Time at her side. He was a burglar and her peace of mind was a house he broke into whenever it pleased him.

"Ricky Bellamy is one screwed up kid."

"That's because he really is an oracle. Don't you understand anything? He was put on this planet to absorb the ugliness in life so the rest of us could live in harmony."

"He's an asshole. Isn't it strange how things worked out? Look at us. We're broke ass refugees on the run. Messing with him was a stupid mistake."

"It wasn't wrong."

"The fuck it wasn't. He tore our lives apart. He caused living hell. Nobody needs that crap."

"Ricky has a unique talent. We should be thankful for it."

"That's bullshit, Rita. Total bullshit. He has an illness."

All of a sudden 2-Time saw me walking down the bus aisle toward him. With each step, the Zegna's ragged hem flapped around my kneecaps. My mouth was set in a petulant moue.

"2-Time! You owe me money!"

"Fuck, dude! I don't owe you a thing!"

2-Time's mind, addled by Life, was playing tricks on him. I wasn't there, nobody was, only the piled up memories of the preceding days, the easy moments and hard moments in 2-Time's benighted life.

FORTY-ONE

The Fukushima waste mass made landfall in Berkeley, right by the interstate freeway. Drivers could see it from the road. Witnesses said they smelled it from a mile away. The Highway Patrol was rerouting traffic south toward Fremont.

I got to the Emergency Management Center's command post on Tuesday evening, a half hour past my appointed time. Lackner met me in the doorway, his gray face seamed with rage. He raised a hand, index finger pointed at my head.

"You're a fucking fraud, Bellamy. You said more airborne contamination was gonna strike today. Then it didn't. Do you know how many millions of dollars we lost on this fiasco?"

He should've been happy there was no more contamination. But what did I expect? I let people boss me around, and when things got funky, as they inevitably did, I danced in limbo.

"C'mon, man, relax."

"You fucked up very badly. You're fired."

"For what?"

"Criminal malfeasance."

"What does that mean?"

"It means you're going to jail."

"Am I getting any severance pay?"

"No."

My self-esteem was shattered. The one skill I had was gone again. Like Heller once said, I was a failed oracle. This was the moment I had been waiting for, the punctuation to my shitty life. It didn't matter that I used to see the future. I was a has-been. My name had become a lesion. I wasn't going to Jerusalem.

Lackner shrilled into his intercom, "I want security personnel up here. On the double."

That was my cue. I cut and ran into the corridor, my sore leg following my good one. I cantered down a staircase to the ground floor lobby and then out the main entrance. I hauled ass to the corner of Turk and Laguna, new condominiums in front of me, the Page Street projects on my right, and hightailed it to the closest bus stop on Market Street.

Three hours later I got to Guadalupe Terrace. The Hondurans' bungalow was sectioned off from the lane by yellow crime scene tape. The bungalow's chimney, the only part of it standing, was girdled by burnt redwood beams, hydro lamps, charred pipes, and wiring.

At Spike's house the porch was bare. The sofa and chairs were gone. The outside walls had been repainted primer white. The broken windows had new panes of glass. The garbage was swept up and stashed in plastic bags, two rows of them by the front steps. A "for sale" sign was planted in the lawn.

Spike had been evicted.

I wished I was young again with no bullet in my head. I drew my coat around me, but I could find no solace in the cashmere's pungent familiarity, my sad and sorry magic cape. In utter misery, I fell to my knees and howled until my throat was raw and all the sorrow in the world was squeezed out of my heart. Shadows swarmed around me, shadows that hardened into death's saccharine white light. I saw the last time I took a tab of Life, the chalky double-barreled pill dissolving on my tongue, the head rush hitting seconds later, inducing a nosebleed, killing the contamination in me. I saw the afternoons at Branch's house, when Doolan went to the Kaiser hospital on Geary Boulevard to re-up his morphine prescription. Branch was drinking port at his office desk, saying: "I fucked up."

And then I fainted. From the Hunters Point shipyard to Islais Creek Channel, to the downtown skyscrapers and the North Beach cafes, over Grace Cathedral and south to Mission Dolores, the Fillmore and Haight-Ashbury, the city looked at me, but all I saw was the white light.